ENGLISH IS NOT EASY

英文給它
有點難

我靠畫畫搞定它

露琪·古提耶雷茲（Luci Gutierrez） 著 歐罷 譯

目錄

這世界上有兩種人：學語言如魚得水的人和水深火熱的人。我（可能還有你）是屬於後面那一組。我甚至不願去想那些花在努力學英文上的時間（和金錢！），那時我其實每分每秒都痛恨英文。但是，會說英文的人看起來好聰明，所以我就繼續學了。那也就代表：上線上課程、暑期密集課程，甚至去到紐約，在冰天凍地的早晨一大早起床，前往布魯克林的俄羅斯區，那邊對我而言就像遙遠的西部一樣。我在時代廣場上課時，很少是清醒的，上課的老師口音又很奇怪，他們還接受日本學生熱心的按摩服務。以上這些經驗每一段都有相對應的課本，談一些像是極限運動、大氣條件這種嚇人的主題，你知道，就是一些你出門看到跳傘的人被颱風吹走時會用到的字彙。

但是，在學了那些之後，我又來到大西洋的另一邊，我得找個方法，即使是用我那忘性很強的記性，也要把學會的東西記住，因此我決定用我的插畫技能來幫助自己背單字和文法概念。而那些圖畫就變成了這本書，學英文也變成了有趣的事。或許這對你不管用，但畫這一頁頁的圖，幫我把英文中一些字串了起來。現在我看起來很聰明吧？

lesson

THE
ENGLISH ALPHABET
[英文字母]

I am
a cauliflower
and I can spell it:
CEE-A-U-EL-I-EF
EL-O-DOUBLE-U-
E-AR

我是一顆花椰菜，而且我會拼這個字：
c·a·u·l·i·f·l·o·w·e·r

A A [eɪ]

B BEE [biː]

C CEE [siː]

D DEE [diː]

E E [iː]

F EF [ɛf]

G GEE [dʒiː]

H AITCH [eɪtʃ]

I i [aɪ]

J JAY [dʒeɪ]

K KAY [keɪ]

L EL [ɛl]

M EM [ɛm]

N EN [ɛn]

O O [oʊ]

P PEE [piː]

Q CUE [kjuː]

R AR [ar]

S ESS [ɛs]

T TEE [tiː]

U U [juː]

V VEE [viː]

W DOUBLE-U [ˈdʌbəlju]

X EX [ɛks]

Y WY [waɪ]

Z ZEE [zē]

SUBJECT
PRONOUNS
［ 主詞代名詞 ］

人稱		代名詞
單數	第一人稱	*I*
	第二人稱	*You*
	第三人稱陽性	*He*
	第三人稱陰性	*She*
	第三人稱中性	*It*
複數	第一人稱	*We*
	第二人稱	*You*
	第三人稱	*They*

主詞代名詞指的是我們在談論的人或事物。

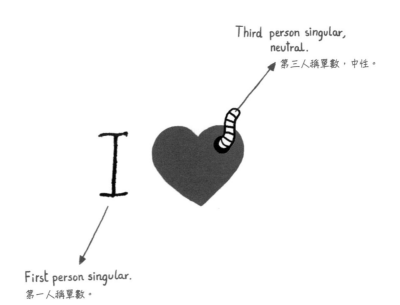

Third person singular,
neutral.
第三人稱單數，中性。

First person singular.
第一人稱單數。

[be 動詞]

be 動詞表示存在。

I AM SMALL.
I AM IN NEW YORK.

我好渺小。
我在紐約。

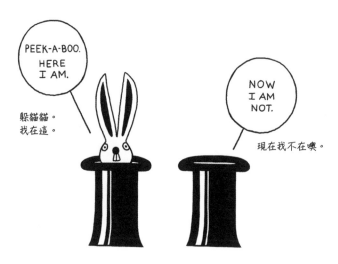

to be
in the
Present
Simple
[be 動詞
的現在簡單式]

be 動詞的**現在簡單式**

I am | I'm
You are | You're
He is | He's
She is | She's
It is | It's
We are | We're
You are | You're
They are | They're

要用否定時，
在 be 動詞後面加 not。

I am not | I'm not
You are not | You aren't
He is not | He isn't
She is not | She isn't
It is not | It isn't
We are not | We aren't
You are not | You aren't
They are not | They aren't

要用**疑問**時，
將主詞和動詞交換位置。

Am I ... ?
Are you ... ?
Is he ... ?
Is she ... ?
Is it ... ?
Are we ... ?
Are you ... ?
Are they ... ?

［表地方的介系詞］

Place
PREPOSITIONS

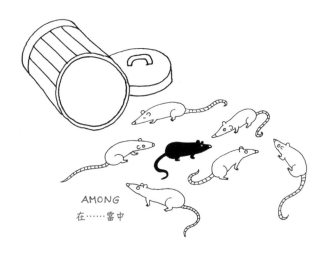

AMONG
在……當中

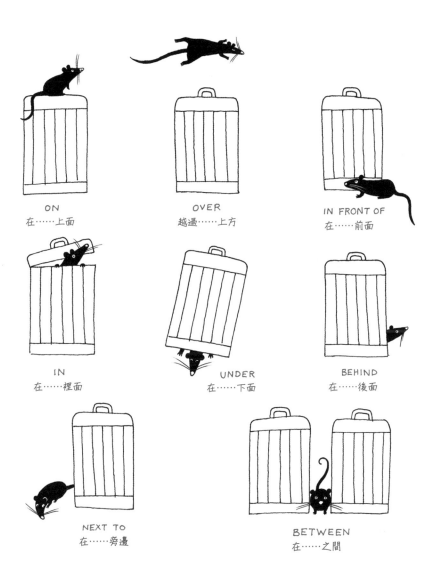

ON
在……上面

OVER
越過……上方

IN FRONT OF
在……前面

IN
在……裡面

UNDER
在……下面

BEHIND
在……後面

NEXT TO
在……旁邊

BETWEEN
在……之間

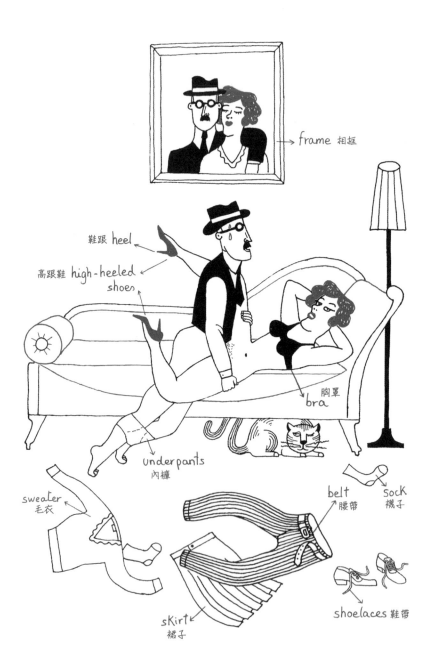

frame 相框

鞋跟 heel

高跟鞋 high-heeled shoes

胸罩 bra

underpants 內褲

sweater 毛衣

belt 腰帶

sock 襪子

skirt 裙子

shoelaces 鞋帶

Where Is It?

在哪裡？

The lamp is <u>next to</u> the chaise lounge.

檯燈在貴妃椅旁邊。

The cat is <u>under</u> the chaise lounge.

貓在貴妃椅下面。

The pants are <u>in front of</u> the cat.

褲子在貓前面。

The picture is <u>behind</u> the chaise lounge.

畫在貴妃椅後面。

Mr. Sweat is <u>in</u> Mrs. Sweat.

斯威特先生在斯威特太太裡面。

WHERE ARE THESE PEOPLE FROM ?
[這些人是打哪兒來的？]

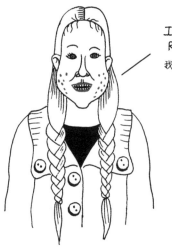

QUESTION
Words
[疑問詞]

Where is he from?
他是哪裡人？

Who is he?
他是誰？

What's his address?
他家地址是什麼？

What's his name?
他叫什麼名字？

What's his phone number?
他的電話是幾號？

How much does he earn?
他賺多少錢？

What's he like?
他是什麼樣的人？

What does he do?
他的工作是什麼？

How old is he?
他幾歲？

What is he into?
他的興趣什麼？

疑問詞用來詢問資訊，而且要有「是」或「不是」之外的答案。

疑問詞	用來問
WHAT 什麼	關於某事的資訊 *What's his name?* 他叫什麼名字？
WHEN 什麼時候	時間 *When is he coming?* 他什麼時候要來？
WHERE 哪裡	地點 *Where is he from?* 他來自哪裡？
WHO 誰	人 *Who is he?* 他是誰？
WHY 為什麼	原因 *Why do you like him?* 你為什麼喜歡他？
HOW 怎麼	方法 *How is he in bed?* 他在床上表現如何？
WHICH 哪個	選擇 *Which one do you like?* 你喜歡哪一個？
WHOSE 誰的	擁有權 *Whose bag is this?* 這個袋子是誰的？
WHOM 誰	哪個人 *Whom are you going to date?* 你要跟誰約會？
HOW MUCH | HOW MANY 多少	數量 *How much does he earn?* 他賺多少錢？
HOW COME 為什麼	原因（why的口語用法） *How come he doesn't call me?* 他為什麼不打電話給我？

如果疑問詞是**介系詞**的受詞，要把介系詞放在最後。

Where is he <u>from</u>? or *What did he come <u>for</u>?*

他從哪裡來？　　或　　　他為什麼來？

WORD ORDER IN SENTENCES
[句子中的字詞順序]

positive SENTENCES
肯定句

主詞	+ 動詞	+ 間接受詞	+ 直接受詞	+ 地點	+ 時間
They	*will give*	*you*	*a terrible beating*	*at school*	*tomorrow.*

他們明天在學校會狠狠揍你一頓。

I	*wish*	*you*	*the best.*

祝你順利。

questions
疑問句

疑問詞	+ 助動詞	+ 主詞	+ 動詞	+ 間接受詞
Why	*did*	*you*	*send*	*him*

為什麼你每天都寄一封匿名信到他的辦公室？

Where	*were*	*you*	—	—

謀殺案發當晚你人在哪裡？

negative SENTENCES
否定句

主詞	+ 動詞	+ 間接受詞	+ 直接受詞	+ 地點	+ 時間
She	*didn't tell*	*him*	*the truth*	*at the pub*	*yesterday.*

她沒跟他講昨天在夜店裡發生的實情。

| *He* | *won't trust* | *her* | _ | _ | *anymore.* |

他不會再相信她了。

跟肯定句一樣的，但否定句需要用助動詞和「not」（be 動詞除外）。

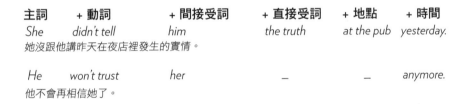

+ 直接受詞	+ 地點	+ 時間
anonymous letters	*to his office*	*every day?*

| | | *the night of the murder?* |

在疑問句中，助動詞（或主要動詞 be 動詞）放在主詞前面，疑問詞則放在句首。

lesson

SIMPLE PRESENT

[現在簡單式]

主詞 + 動詞
You need...
你需要……

YOU NEED a boyfriend that SAYS to you `I LOVE YOU, baby`

你需要一個男朋友對你說：「我愛你，寶貝。」

現在簡單式用來陳述現在時間。
用在永恆為真的不變事實：*The night is dark.* 夜晚是黑的。
用在現在為真的事實：*I feel happy.* 我覺得開心。
用在習慣行為：*I get up late.* 我都起得晚。

下一班火車凌晨一點抵達。
等待的時間享用找吧。

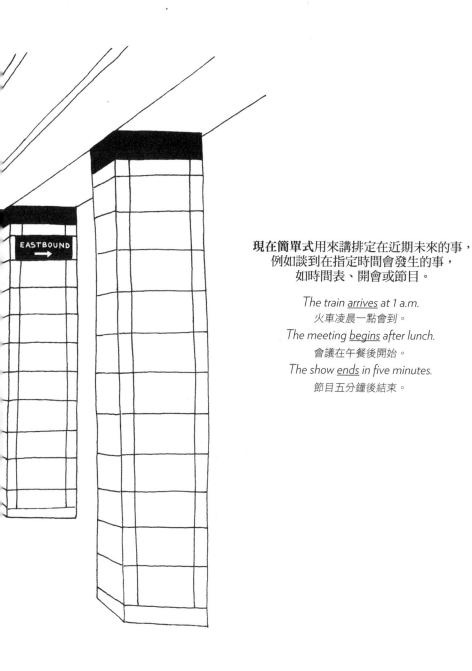

EASTBOUND
→

現在簡單式用來講排定在近期未來的事，
例如談到在指定時間會發生的事，
如時間表、開會或節目。

The train <u>arrives</u> at 1 a.m.
火車凌晨一點會到。
The meeting <u>begins</u> after lunch.
會議在午餐後開始。
The show <u>ends</u> in five minutes.
節目五分鐘後結束。

NEGATIVE
否定

寫現在簡單式的否定，要用：
主詞 + don't | doesn't + 原型動詞

I don't like...
我不喜歡……

DO + NOT = DON'T | DOES + NOT = DOESN'T

I DON'T LIKE PEOPLE.
我不喜歡人。

QUESTION
問句

寫現在簡單式的問句，要用：
Do | Does + 主詞 + 原型動詞

Do you read?
你看書嗎？

DO YOU WORK？
你工作嗎？

NO, I DON'T.
不，我不工作。

DO YOU LIKE MUSIC？
你喜歡音樂嗎？

NO, I DON'T.
不，我不喜歡。

DO YOU GO TO MOVIES？
你看電影嗎？

NO, I DON'T.
不，我不看。

DO YOU READ？
你看書嗎？

NO, I DON'T.
不，我不看。

DO YOU LIKE TRAVELING？
你喜歡旅行嗎？

NO, I DON'T.
不，我不喜歡。

OKAY. DO YOU WANT TO GO TO BED WITH ME？
好吧。那你想跟我上床嗎？

YES, I DO！
想，我想！

［現在簡單式中的第三人稱單數］

現在簡單式中，第三人稱單數 (he, she, it) 動詞後面加 s

I look great. 我看起來不錯。
You look great. 你看起來很棒。
<u>*He looks great.*</u> 他看起來很帥。
<u>*She looks great.*</u> 她看起來很美。
<u>*It looks great.*</u> 這看來挺不賴的。
We look great. 我們看起來不錯。
You look great. 你們看起來很棒。
They look great. 他們看起來很棒。

動詞字尾為 o 的加 es: *do - does.*
動詞字尾為 s 的加 es: *kiss - kisses.*
動詞字尾為 x 的加 es: *mix - mixes.*
動詞字尾為 ch 的加 es: *catch - catches.*
動詞字尾為 sh 的加 es: *push - pushes.*
動詞字尾為 y 而 y 前面為子音的，則要把 y 改成 ies: *cry - cries.*

用 doesn't 來寫否定句，用 does 來寫問句。

I don't snore.
我不會打呼。

You don't snore.
你不會打呼。

<u>*He doesn't snore.*</u>
他不會打呼。

<u>*She doesn't snore.*</u>
她不會打呼。

<u>*It doesn't snore.*</u>
牠不會打呼。

We don't snore.
我們不會打呼。

You don't snore.
你們不會打呼。

They don't snore.
他們不會打呼。

Do I stink?
我會臭嗎？

Do you stink?
你會臭嗎？

<u>*Does he stink?*</u>
他會臭嗎？

<u>*Does she stink?*</u>
她會臭嗎？

<u>*Does it stink?*</u>
牠會臭嗎？

Do we stink?
我們會臭嗎？

Do you stink?
你們會臭嗎？

Do they stink?
他們會臭嗎？

PLURALS

［複數］

當可數名詞指兩個或以上時，就用那個名詞的複數型。
複數型一般是在名詞加上 s 來構成。

computer - computers（電腦）

phantom - phantoms（鬼魅）

umbrella - umbrellas（雨傘）

house - houses（房子）

book - books（書本）

hat - hats（帽子）

有些名詞不太一樣。
這些是最常見的例外。

名詞字尾是：

O, S, X, ZZ, CH, SH, 加 ES:

potato - potatoes（馬鈴薯）
kiss - kisses（親吻）
box - boxes（箱子）
buzz - buzzes（嗡嗡聲）
witch - witches（女巫）
dish - dishes（盤子）

名詞字尾是 Z, 加 ZES.

quiz - quizzes（小考）

有些名詞字尾為 O, 加 S.

photo - photos（相片）
piano - pianos（鋼琴）

子音以 Y 結尾, Y 改成 IES.

city - cities（城市）

大部分名詞字尾是 F 或 FE 的, 改成 VES.

wolf - wolves（狼）

大部分名詞字尾是 IS 的, 改成 ES.

crisis - crises（危機）

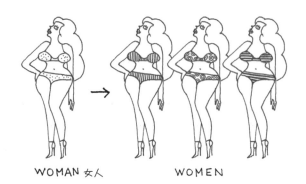

WOMAN 女人   WOMEN

IRREGULAR PLURALS
[不規則複數型]

不規則名詞不適用前面的規則。
這些是最常見的。

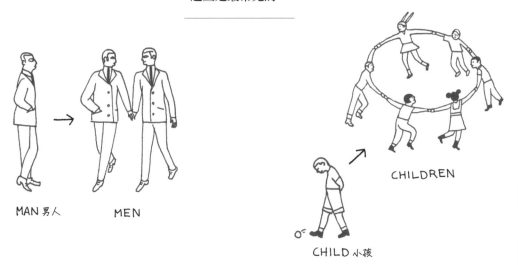

MAN 男人   MEN

CHILDREN

CHILD 小孩

FOOT 腳 → FEET

SHEEP 羊 → SHEEP

TOOTH 牙齒 → TEETH

PERSON 人 → PEOPLE

MOUSE 老鼠 → MICE

COUNTABLE
AND
UNCOUNTABLE
NOUNS
[可數名詞和不可數名詞]

可數名詞前面可以有數字，
也有複數型：

3 years, 2 suitcases, 1 rabbit
三年　兩卡皮箱　一隻兔子

不可數名詞前面不可以有數字，
也沒有複數型：

air, water, oil, hope
空氣　水　油　希望

ARTICLES WITH COUNTABLE AND UNCOUNTABLE NOUNS

A | AN, THE

可數名詞 & 不可數名詞的冠詞
a/an 和 the

可數名詞的冠詞這麼用：

加 a | an
是在第一次用那個名詞時。

There is <u>a naked man</u> in the garden.
花園裡有個裸男

a- 用在名詞開頭是子音的時候：*a friend*（朋友）
an- 用在名詞開頭是母音的時候：*an egg*（蛋）

加 the 是在之後使用那個名詞的時候，
或者是對方已經知道你在指什麼的時候。

<u>*The naked man*</u> *is dancing.*
那個裸男在跳舞。

不加冠詞是你在指一般狀況時。

I don't like <u>children</u>.
我不喜歡小孩。

不可數名詞的冠詞這麼用：

不加冠詞：若你是指那東西的
全部或任何一個。

I don't need <u>help</u>.
我不需要幫助。

加 the：當你指特定實例時。

Thanks for <u>the help</u> you didn't give me before.
謝謝你先前沒幫到的那個忙。

HOW MUCH | HOW MANY
[有多少]

用 how much?（有多少？）
來問**不可數**的東西。

用 how many?（有多少？）
來問**可數**的東西。

1 money（一個錢）
2 money（兩個錢）
3 moneys（三個錢）

1 orange（一顆橘子）
2 oranges（兩顆橘子）
3 oranges（三顆橘子）

[一些和任何]

some（一些）和 any（任何）
用在說話者沒有特定指一個數字或精確的數量。

some 用在肯定句

加不可數名詞：
You have <u>some butter</u> on your nose. 你鼻子上有些奶油。
加複數可數名詞：
You have <u>some boogers</u> in your nose. 你鼻子裡有些鼻屎。

any 用在否定句和疑問句

加不可數名詞：
I don't want <u>any risk</u> in my life. 我不想冒任何生命危險。
加複數可數名詞：
Do you have <u>any friends</u>? 你有任何朋友嗎？

這些規則有兩個常見的例外：

提議或要求的問句時，用 some：
Would you like <u>some more tea</u>, darling? 親愛的，你還要再喝些茶嗎？

表示「哪一個都沒關係」時，可以在肯定句中用 any：
You can call me <u>at any time</u>. 你隨時都可以打給我。

THERE IS THERE ARE

[有]

there is 和 there are 用來講某事物存在或不存在。

there is 用在單數的主詞。
there are 用在複數的主詞。

There is an ice rink. 那邊有一座溜冰場。

There are a lot of buildings. 那邊有很多建築物。

There are no trees. 那邊沒有樹。

There is no King Kong. 沒有金剛啦。

Are there any school buses? 有校車嗎？

Yes, there are. 有，有的。

Are there people skating? 有人在溜冰嗎？

Yes, there is a guy skating on an ice rink 有，有一個人在溜冰場溜冰。

and there is a girl skating on a building. 還有一個女孩在建築物上溜冰。

Is there a businessman in a hurry? 有趕時間的生意人嗎？

No, there isn't. 不，沒有。

Demonstratives
THiS · THESE · THAT · THOSE
[指示詞：這個、這些、那個、那些]

指示詞用來顯示與說話者的距離。
距離可以是心理層面的，也可以是實體層面的。

this（這個）：指附近的單數名詞
these（這些）：指附近的複數名詞
that（那個）：指遠處的單數名詞
those（那些）：指遠處的複數名詞

指示詞可以當作：

代名詞	形容詞
<u>This</u> is the dead tree. 這就是那棵死掉的樹。	<u>This</u> tree is dead. 這棵樹死掉了。
I don't like <u>that</u>. 我不喜歡那個。	I came in <u>that</u> car. 我坐那輛車來的。
<u>These</u> are mine. 這些是我的。	I left <u>these</u> garbage bags. 我留下了這些垃圾袋。
<u>Those</u> are my neighbors. 那些是我的鄰居。	<u>Those</u> guys are unpleasant. 那些傢伙很討人厭。

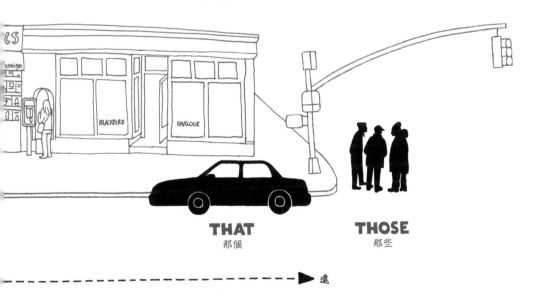

THAT
那個

THOSE
那些

遠

POSSESSIVES
PRONOUNS AND ADJECTIVES
[所有格：代名詞和形容詞]

主詞代名詞	所有格代名詞	所有格形容詞
I 我	mine 我的	my 我的
you 你	yours 你的	your 你的
he 他	his 他的	his 他的
she 她	hers 她的	her 她的
it 它	its 它的	its 它的
we 我們	ours 我們的	our 我們的
you 你們	yours 你們的	your 你們的
they 他們	theirs 他們的	their 他們的

所有格代名詞用來代替名詞

Peggy's dress is pink. Mine is black.
佩姬的洋裝是粉紅色的。我的是黑色的。

**所有格形容詞通常用來形容名詞，
而且像其他形容詞一樣，放在名詞前面。**

My dress is nicer than her dress.
我的洋裝比她的洋裝漂亮。

VIVIAN'S HUSBAND IS
EVERY WOMAN'S DREAM HUSBAND.
薇薇安的老公是每個女人的理想老公。

'S

+ NOUNS
[名詞的所有格 's]

單數名詞加 's 表示擁有：

I don't like my sister's boyfriend. 我不喜歡我妹妹的男朋友。

's 可以用在規則複數名詞：

I love ladies' shoes. 我喜歡女鞋。

或不規則複數名詞：

I don't care about men's shoes. 我不在乎男鞋。

還有用在名字

Kate's dog barks every night. 凱特的狗每天晚上都會叫。
Do you have Susan's phone number? 你有蘇珊的電話號碼嗎？

如果名字字尾是 s，把它當作跟其他任何單數名詞一樣，加 's。

Don't eat Charles's breakfast. 不要吃查爾斯的早餐。

lesson 3

VOCABULARY:
The Body and Stuff
[字彙：身體和有的沒有的]

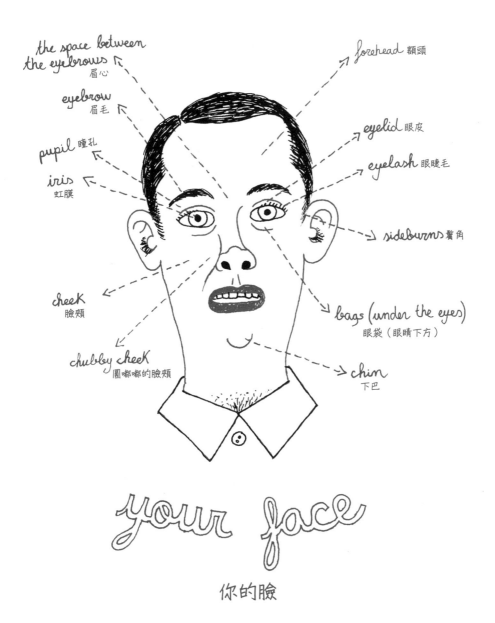

the space between
the eyebrows
眉心

eyebrow
眉毛

pupil 瞳孔

iris
虹膜

cheek
臉頰

chubby cheek
圓嘟嘟的臉頰

forehead 額頭

eyelid 眼皮

eyelash 眼睫毛

sideburns 鬢角

bags (under the eyes)
眼袋（眼睛下方）

chin
下巴

your face

你的臉

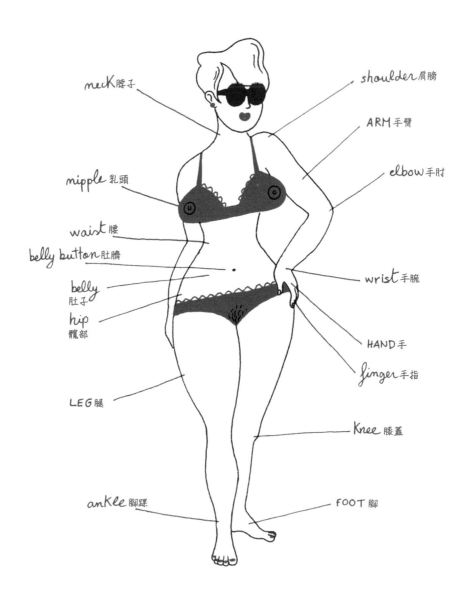

neck 脖子

shoulder 肩膀

ARM 手臂

elbow 手肘

nipple 乳頭

waist 腰

belly button 肚臍

belly 肚子

hip 髖部

wrist 手腕

HAND 手

finger 手指

LEG 腿

Knee 膝蓋

ankle 腳踝

FOOT 腳

你可以看到她的 boobs（奶子）和她的 lady parts（私處）！真不害臊！！！

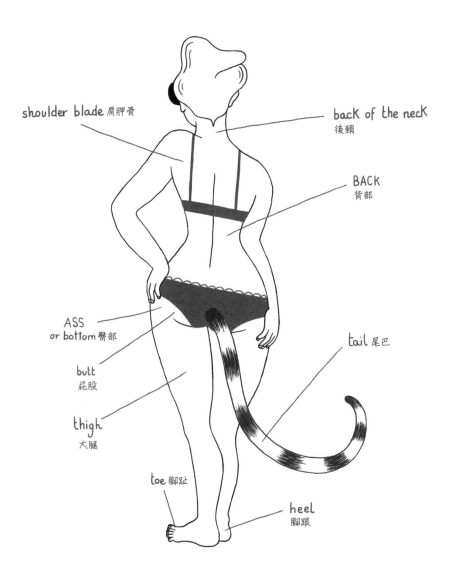

shoulder blade 肩胛骨

back of the neck
後頸

BACK
背部

ASS
or bottom 臀部

butt
屁股

tail 尾巴

thigh
大腿

toe 腳趾

heel
腳跟

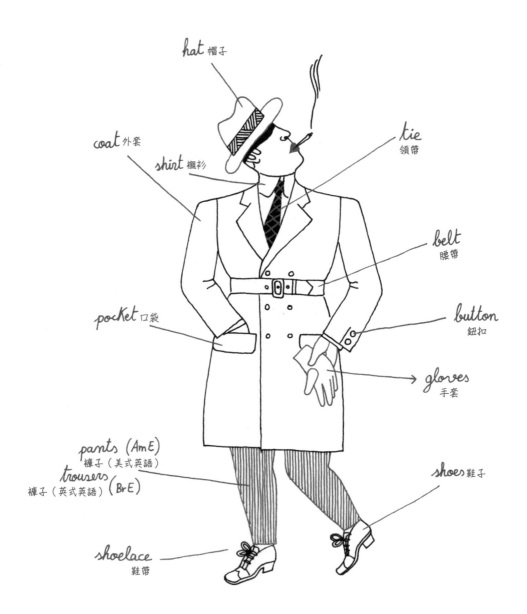

hat 帽子

coat 外套

shirt 襯衫

tie 領帶

belt 腰帶

pocket 口袋

button 鈕扣

gloves 手套

pants (AmE)
褲子（美式英語）
trousers
褲子（英式英語）(BrE)

shoes 鞋子

shoelace
鞋帶

VOCABULARY *for an elegant man*
紳士相關字彙

男人身體的字彙跟女人身體是一樣的，
但是有一些不同之處，包括：

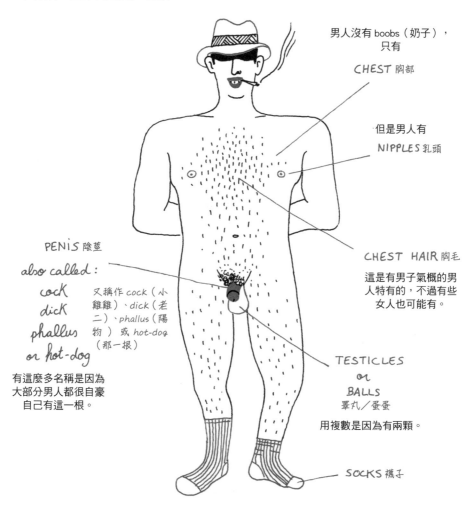

男人沒有 boobs（奶子），
只有

CHEST 胸部

但是男人有
NIPPLES 乳頭

CHEST HAIR 胸毛

這是有男子氣概的男人特有的，不過有些女人也可能有。

PENIS 陰莖
also called:
cock
dick
phallus
or hot-dog

又稱作 cock（小雞雞）、dick（老二）、phallus（陽物）或 hot-dog（那一根）

有這麼多名稱是因為大部分男人都很自豪自己有這一根。

TESTICLES
or
BALLS
睪丸／蛋蛋

用複數是因為有兩顆。

SOCKS 襪子

VOCABULARY for the man's body
男人身體相關字彙

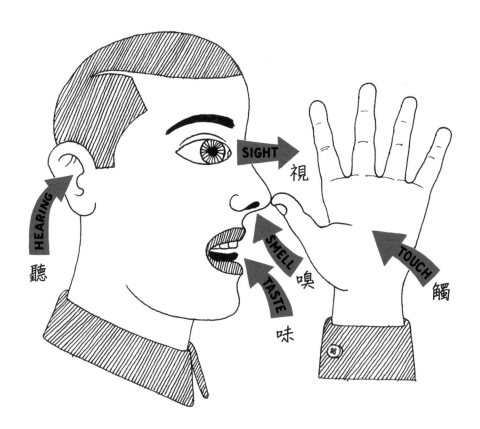

The 5 Senses

[五感]

你可以透過五感來享樂，只要你沒有任何殘疾。

My sense of <u>smell</u> is almost non-existent.
我的嗅覺幾乎不存在。

I have refined <u>taste.</u>
我的味覺很靈敏。

His <u>touch</u> is unpleasant.
他的觸摸很不舒服。

Speak up! My <u>hearing</u> is getting worse.
說大聲一點！我的聽覺越來越差了。

She fell in love at first <u>sight</u>.
她第一眼就陷入愛河了。

JOBS

[職業]

是我們為了賺錢而做的事。

在職業前面加冠詞 **a | an**
I'm a waitress.
我是女服務生。

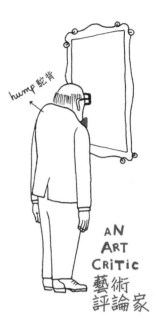

AN ART CRITIC
藝術評論家

chocolate 巧克力
strawberry jam 草莓果醬

A PASTRY CHEF
糕點師傅

hump 駝背

A HOTEL ATTENDANT
飯店櫃檯服務人員

A PIANIST
鋼琴家

cap 帽子

A MOBSTER
匪徒

Wait outside！在外面等！

A WAITRESS
女服務生

A BUTCHER 屠夫

sweet
sausage
糯米腸

A HOMELESS PERSON 流浪漢

grandmother 祖母
granddaughter 孫女
mother-in-law 婆婆（岳母）
daugter-in-law 媳婦
son 兒子
brother 兄弟
wife 妻子
husband 丈夫
wife 妻子
father 父親
daughter 女兒
sister 姊妹
mother 母親

MADELEINE
梅德琳

CARRIE
凱莉

PHIL
菲爾

ELISA
艾莉莎

JOHN
約翰

SUE
蘇

family
［家庭］

Carrie and Phil got married 24 years ago. John, their son, is 24 years old. Carrie and Phil usually say he was conceived on their wedding night, but the family knows it was before. Elisa is a rebellious teenager. She is 14 years old. She hates to spend time with her family. She wants to be different and, more than anything, she doesn't want to be like her mother. Elisa has a sister-in-law, Sue, who has brought a new baby into the family and the new tradition of barbecuing on Sundays. The grandparents are in love with little Madeleine, as is John, but there is something they don't know: John is not really her father.

That's a little family secret.

凱莉和菲爾二十四年前結婚的。他們的兒子約翰二十四歲。凱莉和菲爾常會説他是在他們的新婚夜懷上的，但家人都知道是在結婚前有的。艾莉莎是個叛逆的少女，她十四歲，討厭跟家人相處，不想和他們一樣，尤其是不想像她媽一樣。艾莉莎有一個大嫂，蘇，她為這個家帶來了一個新生寶寶，還有新的傳統：每週日都要烤肉。這對祖父母很喜歡小梅德琳，約翰也是，不過有件事是他們不知道的：約翰不是她真正的父親。
那是個小小的家庭秘密。

How many siblings do you have?

你有幾個兄弟姊妹呢？

I have 4 siblings.
I have 2 brothers
and 2 sisters.
But I would
prefer to
have
none.

我有四個兄弟姊妹。

我有兩個哥哥和兩個姊姊。

不過我寧願一個都沒有。

at home

[家裡]

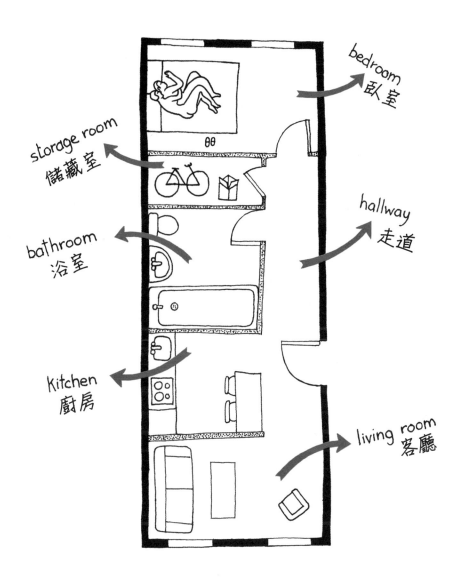

bedroom
臥室

storage room
儲藏室

hallway
走道

bathroom
浴室

kitchen
廚房

living room
客廳

Let's Eat!

[開動吧！]

8 A.M. *Breakfast*
早上八點吃早餐

12 P.M. *Lunch*
下午十二點吃午餐

ANY TIME! *Snack*
任何時候都可以吃點心

7 P.M. Dinner

晚上七點吃晚餐

菜單
= MENU =
★ STARTERS ★ 前菜

- APPETIZERS
開胃菜

- SOUPS
湯

- SALADS 沙拉

- SANDWICHES
三明治

- PASTA) 義大利麵

★ MAIN COURSES ★ 主菜

- FISH 魚

- SEAFOOD
海鮮

MEATS 肉類

CHICKEN
雞肉

PORK
豬肉

BEEF
牛肉

- SIDE 小菜
DISHES

★ DESSERTS ★ 甜點

★ BEVERAGES ★ 飲品

WINES
紅酒

SODAS
汽水

BEERS
啤酒

french fries
薯條

burger
漢堡

cheeseburger
起士漢堡

chicken wings
雞翅

hot dog
熱狗

sausage
香腸

pretzel
胡椒捲餅

FOOD
Vocabulary
[食物字彙]

fried egg
煎蛋

noodles
麵

omelet 蛋捲

chips
洋芋片

olive oil
橄欖油

onion
rings
洋蔥圈

pepperoni pizza
經典義式辣香腸披薩

salt & pepper
鹽 & 胡椒

ketchup & mustard
番茄醬 & 芥末醬

sushi
壽司

bread
麵包

mashed potatoes
薯泥

cheese
起士

loaf of
bread
一條吐司

pickles
醃醬瓜

jam
果醬

marshmallows
棉花糖

cookie
餅乾

butter
奶油

sugar
糖

SKIPPY

croissant
可頌麵包

donut
甜甜圈

peanut butter
花生醬

cheesecake
起士蛋糕

muffin
英式鬆餅

seafood
海鮮

shrimp
蝦子

mussels
貽貝

vegetables
蔬菜

onion
洋蔥

parsley
香菜

peas
豆子

tomato
番茄

cucumber
黃瓜

mushrooms
蘑菇

lettuce
萵苣

garlic
大蒜

asparagus
蘆筍

eggplant
茄子

artichoke
朝鮮薊

carrot
紅蘿蔔

green beans
青豆

red pepper
紅椒

fruit
水果

peach
桃子

watermelon
西瓜

coconut
椰子

pear
梨子

pineapple
鳳梨

lemon
檸檬

strawberry
草莓

banana
香蕉

melon
甜瓜

peanuts
花生

nuts
堅果

almonds
杏仁

walnuts
核桃

hazelnuts
榛果

lesson 4

VOCABULARY VERBS

[動詞字彙]

TO WALK
走路

TO FLY
飛行

TO JUMP
跳躍

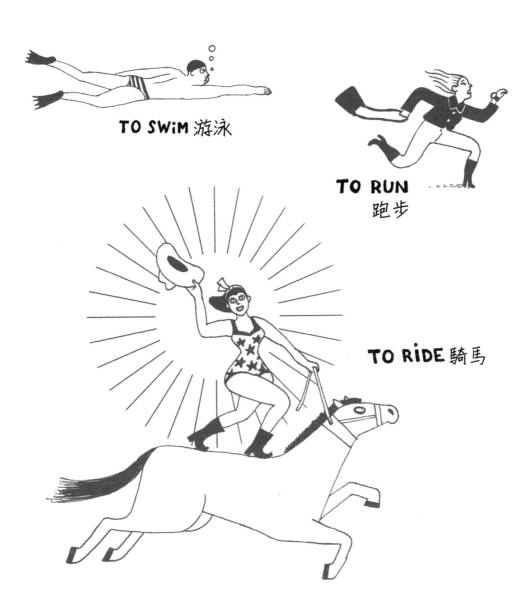

TO SWIM 游泳

TO RUN
跑步

TO RIDE 騎馬

TO ARGUE
爭吵

TO HUG
擁抱

TO THROW
丟

TO REST
休息

TO REALIZE
發現

The day after arguing with his wife, hugging her, getting dishes thrown at him and resting, Jeff realized he was wearing his slippers on the way back home from work.

跟老婆起爭執、抱抱、又被丟盤子,還有休息之後,
隔天傑夫下班回家的路上發現他腳上穿的是拖鞋。

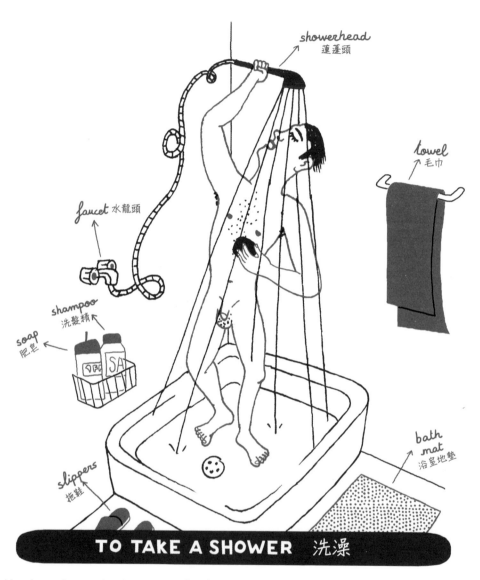

showerhead
蓮蓬頭

towel
毛巾

faucet 水龍頭

shampoo
洗髮精

soap
肥皂

bath
mat
浴室地墊

slippers
拖鞋

TO TAKE A SHOWER 洗澡

He <u>takes a shower</u> when he gets up, after the gym, after having sex and before going to bed. Between showers, he works in an organization that fights global warming.
他在起床時、上健身房後、嘿咻後和睡覺前都會洗澡。在洗澡跟洗澡之間,他在一個對抗全球暖化的機構上班。

TO BRUSH 刷牙

She is a little dirty. She gets dirty even when she <u>brushes</u> her teeth.
她有點髒，甚至連刷牙都會弄髒自己。

TO COMB 梳

He usually <u>combs</u> his hair with gel because his lover likes it.
他通常梳頭會用髮膠，
因為他的愛人喜歡這樣。

TO WEAR 穿戴

He <u>wears</u> this hat and these glasses to feel like a more interesting person.
他會戴帽子和眼鏡，
這樣會覺得自己是個比較有趣的人。

TO UNDO 打開

She <u>is undoing</u> the buttons of her shirt to do a striptease for her gynecologist.
她打開襯衫的扣子，
要跳脫衣舞給她的婦科醫生看。

你可以對一隻腳做的一些事

DAYDREAM

做白日夢

to
CHEW
嚼口香糖

Tim was a sensitive and delicate boy. His classmates used to laugh at him. One day after school, Tim was shot by a slingshot*. He lost an eye. Ever since that day, Tim walks around school with a hole in his face, <u>chewing</u> and blowing what looks like his lost eye. Now, Tim is every kid's nightmare.

提姆是個敏感又纖弱的男孩。他的同學以前都會取笑他。有一天放學後,提姆被彈弓打到,就少了一隻眼睛。自那天起,提姆就臉上有個洞地在學校晃蕩,還一邊嚼口香糖、一邊吹看起來很像他不見的那隻眼睛的泡泡。如今,提姆是每個孩子的夢魘。

*

GET tired
「變得」疲倦

GET the bus
「趕上」公車

GET

得到；變成；趕上；抓住；了解；買

"To get" 有很多意思！

GET wet
「變得」濕掉

GET help
「取得」協助

GET the ball
「抓住」那顆球

GET home
「抵達」家

$E=mc^2$

GET the lesson
「了解」那堂課

GET groceries
「買」雜貨

GET a letter
「收到」一封信

the IMPERATIVE
[祈使句]
用動詞但不加代名詞

用來下直接命令
Take your hands off my legs.
把你的雙手拿開，別碰我的腿。

用在標語和通知
Do not touch.
請勿碰觸。

用來指路
Carry on when you get to the edge.
走到邊邊時，繼續走下去。

用來給非正式的建議
Tell him how much you hate him.
告訴他你有多討厭他。

用來邀請
Sit closer, please.
請坐靠近一點。

Stand clear of the closing doors, please.

門將關閉時，請站離遠一點。

IF YOU SEE SOMETHING, SAY SOMETHING.

如果你看到什麼，說點什麼吧。

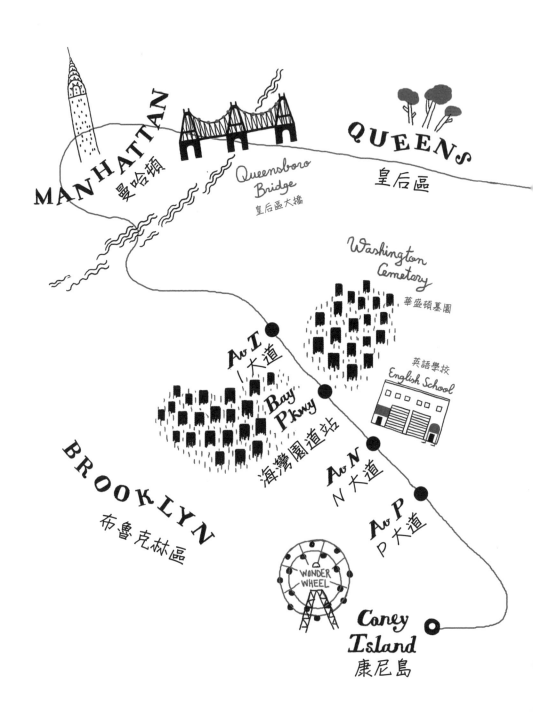

F 線之詩

the Ⓕ line poem

Take the F line to Brooklyn 布魯克林區搭F線可以到
if you are lucky, you'll arrive in the evening. 如果運氣好，晚上就會到。
Let's go to Avenue N 我們來去N大道
where English class will never end. 英文課的盡頭永遠看不到。
Go past Avenue I 經過I大道
then Bay Parkway you'll see with your eyes. 然後就會看到海灣園道。
Don't miss the cemetery from the train! 搭地鐵墓園別漏掉！
Next stop is Avenue N! 下一站就是N大道
but suddenly you are on Avenue P. 但你又突然到了P大道。
Isn't Avenue N where you should be? 你不是應該要去N大道？
The F line is unpredictable F線真是難預料
from local to express service, it's quite variable. 從地方線到快捷線，變來變去找不到。
Get back on the F line to Manhattan 去曼哈頓再回到F線這一條
if you don't want to take a walk on Coney Island. 如果不想漫步康尼島。
So _wait_ for the next train on Avenue P 就在P大道等下一班車到
your frozen nose you will see. 凍僵的鼻子你會看到。
Hey! Not so bad, the F train is coming 嘿！沒那麼糟，F線火車就要進站了
but again you miss Avenue N until tomorrow morning. 但是又再錯過N大道，又到隔天一大早。

lesson

我當時也在鐵達尼號上，但不是跟李奧納多‧迪卡皮歐在一起。可惡！

to be
in the Simple Past

[be 動詞 的過去簡單式]

be 動詞的**過去簡單式**

I was
You were
He was
She was
It was
We were
You were
They were

要用否定時，
在 be 動詞的變化型後面加
not。

I was not | I wasn't
You were not | You weren't
He was not | He wasn't
She was not | She wasn't
It was not | It wasn't
We were not | We weren't
You were not | You weren't
They were not | They weren't

要用疑問時，
將主詞和動詞交換位置。

Was I ... ?
Were you ... ?
Was he ... ?
Was she ... ?
Was it ... ?
Were we ... ?
Were you ... ?
Were they ... ?

Simple Past
[過去簡單式]

主詞 + 過去式
She lived...
她那時過著⋯⋯

She <u>was</u> young.
她那時很年輕。
She <u>loved</u> a man. She <u>dreamed.</u>
她愛過一個男人，她夢想著。
She <u>lived</u> through terrible and wonderful things. She <u>sang</u>.
她經歷過可怕的事，也經歷過美好的事。
她唱歌。
And she still does!
而且她現在還在唱！
This is her and her walker.
這是她和她的助行器。

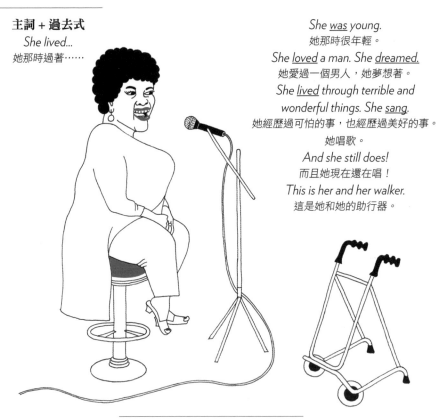

過去簡單式描述過去發生的動作或情況。
用在事件發生在過去時：*My childhood <u>was</u> happy.* 我的童年很快樂。
用在事件完全結束了：*I <u>washed</u> all the dishes.* 我洗好碗了。
用在我們說（或了解）事件的時間、地點：*I <u>woke up</u> in Phil's bed.* 我醒來時在菲爾的床上。

forming
the simple past tense
過去簡單式的構成

過去規則動詞的過去簡單式只要加 **ed** 即可，
不過有些動詞有一點不一樣。

動詞結尾是 e 的加 d：
*live - lived*的（過生活）

是子音+y 的，把 y 改成 i 再加 ed：
cry - cried（哭泣）

是一個母音 + 一個子音的（但不是 w、y），把字尾子音重複後再加ed：
commit - committed（犯；做）

其他的都加 ed
jump - jumped（跳）

VERB + ED

動詞 + ED

negative 否定

寫過去簡單式的否定，要用：
主詞 + did not | didn't + 原型動詞
I didn't go...
我沒去……
DID + NOT = DIDN'T

I didn't go
to school today.
我今天沒去上學。

question 問句

寫過去簡單式的問句，要用：
Did + 主詞 + 原型動詞
Did you love her?
你愛過她嗎？

IRREGULAR VERBS

[不規則動詞]

英文中有許多不規則動詞，過去式不是加 **ed**。

不定詞	過去簡單式	過去分詞	意思
ARISE	AROSE	ARISEN	興起；出現
AWAKE	AWOKE	AWOKEN	叫醒
BE	WAS | WERE	BEEN	是；存在
BEAT	BEAT	BEATEN | BEAT	打；跳動；擊敗；重複地打
BECOME	BECAME	BECOME	變成
BEGIN	BEGAN	BEGUN	開始
BEND	BENT	BENT	弄彎；變彎
BET	BET	BET	賭注
BITE	BIT	BITTEN	咬
BLEED	BLED	BLED	流血
BLOW	BLEW	BLOWN	吹
BREAK	BROKE	BROKEN	弄壞；弄破
BRING	BROUGHT	BROUGHT	帶來

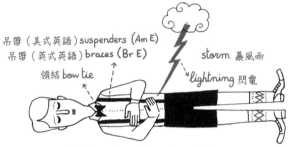

吊帶（美式英語）suspenders (Am E)
吊帶（英式英語）braces (Br E)
領結 bow tie
storm 暴風雨
lightning 閃電

He has a heart but it doesn't <u>beat</u> anymore.
他有一顆心，但不再跳動了。

TO BEAT ♥ BEAT ♥ BEAT ♥ BEATEN ♥
打；跳動；擊敗

TO BURST
BURST - BURST - BURST
爆炸；破裂

TO FEED
FEED FED FED
餵食

不定詞	過去簡單式	過去分詞	意思
BUILD	BUILT	BUILT	建造
BURN	BURNED ｜ BURNT	BURNED ｜ BURNT	燃燒；著火；被火焰摧毀
BURST	BURST	BURST	爆炸；破裂
BUY	BOUGHT	BOUGHT	購買
CATCH	CAUGHT	CAUGHT	捕捉；抓；攔截拿住
CHOOSE	CHOSEN	CHOSEN	選擇
CLING	CLUNG	CLUNG	緊緊抓住
COME	CAME	COME	來
COST	COST	COST	花費；使花錢；具有價值
CREEP	CREPT	CREPT	爬行；緩慢地移動
CUT	CUT	CUT	剪；裁
DEAL	DEALT	DEALT	交易；處理；分配或販賣
DIG	DUG	DUG	挖
DIVE	DIVED ｜ DOVE	DIVED	潛入；潛水
DO	DID	DONE	做；執行
DRAW	DREW	DRAWN	用線條畫畫
DREAM	DREAMED ｜ DREAMT	DREAMED ｜ DREAMT	做夢；夢想
DRINK	DRANK	DRUNK	喝；飲
DRIVE	DROVE	DRIVEN	開車
EAT	ATE	EATEN	吃
FALL	FELL	FALLEN	掉落；跌倒
FEED	FED	FED	餵；給予食物
FEEL	FELT	FELT	感覺
FIGHT	FOUGHT	FOUGHT	打架；爭吵
FIND	FOUND	FOUND	尋找；發現某事物

不定詞	過去簡單式	過去分詞	意思
FIT	FIT | FITTED	FIT	適合；合身
FLEE	FLED	FLED	逃走
FLING	FLUNG	FLUNG	用力丟或拋
FLY	FLEW	FLOWN	飛
FORBID	FORBADE | FORBID	FORBIDDEN	禁止
FORGET	FORGOT	FORGOTTEN	忘記；遺忘
FORGIVE	FORGAVE	FORGIVEN	原諒
FREEZE	FROZE	FROZEN	結冰；冷凍
GET	GOT	GOTTEN | GOT	拿到；取得；收到
GIVE	GAVE	GIVEN	給予
GO	WENT	GONE	去；前往
GRIND	GROUND	GROUND	磨碎
GROW	GREW	GROWN	成長；生長
HANG	HUNG	HUNG	吊掛
HAVE	HAD	HAD	擁有或持有
HEAR	HEARD	HEARD	聽到聲音
HIDE	HID	HIDDEN	隱藏；藏起來
HIT	HIT	HIT	打；擊
HOLD	HELD	HELD	保持；持有
HURT	HURT	HURT	傷害；痛
KEEP	KEPT	KEPT	擁有或保有
KNEEL	KNELT | KNEELED	KNELT | KNEELED	跪
KNIT	KNIT | KNITTED	KNIT | KNITTED	編織
KNOW	KNEW	KNOWN	知道；認識
LAY	LAID	LAID	放；躺；鋪

I forbid you to smoke.
我禁止你抽菸。

TO FORBID
FORBID-FORBADE-FORBIDDEN
禁止

Little Monkey hanged Thomas while he <u>hung</u> from a tree.
小猴子吊死了湯瑪士，牠掛在樹上。

HANG HUNG HUNG
& HANG HANGED HANGED
吊；掛

TO KNIT
KNIT-KNIT|KNITTED-KNIT|KNITTED
編織

He leads the gang.
他帶領那一幫混混 ←

They are easily led.
→ 他們很好指揮

TO LEAD | LEAD LED LED
領導

借

ribbon 緞帶
necklace 項鍊

Mrs. Sharp <u>borrowed</u> a little thing from Mr. Sharp. Mr. Sharp didn't want to <u>lend</u> it to her. She pretended to understand, but she didn't. When night came and the snores of Mr. Sharp got louder, she raised the knife... and cut! Then she could sleep soundly.

夏普太太向夏普先生借了一個小東西。夏普先生不想借給她。她假裝諒解,但其實並不。到了晚上,夏普先生的打呼聲越來越大聲的時候。她拿起刀子……切下去!然後她就可以好好睡覺了。

不定詞	過去簡單式	過去分詞	意思
LEAD	LED	LED	領導；帶領
LEAP	LEAPED | LEAPT	LEAPED | LEAPT	跳躍
LEAVE	LEFT	LEFT	離開或遠離
LEND	LENT	LENT	借出
LET	LET	LET	讓；允許
LIE	LAY	LAIN	躺
LIGHT	LIT | LIGHTED	LIT | LIGHTED	照亮
LOSE	LOST	LOST	輸；失去
MAKE	MADE	MADE	使；做；創作；建造
MEAN	MEANT	MEANT	意思是；打算表達；示意
MEET	MET	MET	會見；相遇
PAY	PAID	PAID	付錢來買物品或服務
PROVE	PROVED	PROVED | PROVEN	證明；證實；呈現事實
PUT	PUT	PUT	放在指定位置
QUIT	QUIT	QUIT	退出；放棄；辭職；中止活動
READ	READ	READ	閱讀
RIDE	RODE	RIDDEN	騎；乘
RING	RANG	RUNG	響；包圍；製造鈴聲
RISE	ROSE	RISEN	興起；起來；增加
RUN	RAN	RUN	跑
SAY	SAID	SAID	說
SEE	SAW	SEEN	看見
SEEK	SOUGHT	SOUGHT	試圖找到；尋找
SELL	SOLD	SOLD	販賣
SEND	SENT	SENT	寄；送

不定詞	過去簡單式	過去分詞	意思
SET	SET	SET	放；設定
SEW	SEWED	SEWED | SEWN	縫合；用針線縫
SHAKE	SHOOK	SHAKEN	搖動；震動
SHAVE	SHAVED	SHAVED | SHAVEN	刮；剃
SHINE	SHONE | SHINED	SHONE | SHINED	發亮；照亮；發光
SHOOT	SHOT	SHOT	發射；開槍
SHOW	SHOWED	SHOWN	展示；顯示
SHRINK	SHRANK | SHRUNK	SHRUNK | SHRUNKEN	縮小；變小
SHUT	SHUT	SHUT	關上；關閉
SING	SANG	SUNG	唱歌
SINK	SANK | SUNK	SUNK	沉沒；下沉
SIT	SAT	SAT | SITTEN	坐
SLEEP	SLEPT	SLEPT	睡覺
SLIDE	SLID	SLID	滑動；滑落
SPEAK	SPOKE	SPOKEN	說話
SPEED	SPED | SPEEDED	SPED | SPEEDED	加速；快速移動
SPEND	SPENT	SPENT	花錢或時間；花費
SPILL	SPILLED | SPILT	SPILLED | SPILT	溢出；濺出
SPIN	SPUN	SPUN	旋轉；快速轉動
SPIT	SPIT | SPAT	SPAT	吐
SPLIT	SPLIT	SPLIT	分開；裂開
SPREAD	SPREAD	SPREAD	展開；散播；打開；延伸
SPRING	SPRANG	SPRUNG	跳；彈起
STAND	STOOD	STOOD	站立
STEAL	STOLE	STOLEN	偷竊

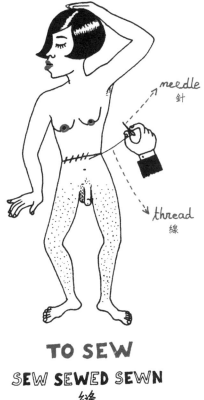

needle
針

thread
線

TO SEW
SEW SEWED SEWN
縫

Mr. Smith <u>sewed</u> half of his pretty neighbor's body and half of his nice butcher's body together. Now he has the perfect wife. Or does he have the perfect husband?

史密斯先生把他那美麗鄰居一半的身體和他那善良屠夫一半的身體縫在一起。現在他有了完美的老婆。還是他有了完美的老公？

TO STICK
STICK·STUCK·STUCK
刺；戳；黏貼

TO STING
STING-STUNG-STUNG
叮；刺；螫

TO SWEEP
SWEEP-SWEPT-SWEPT
打掃；清除

For a good wash, <u>wring</u> tightly.
要好好洗，就要好好擰。

TO WRING
WRING-WRUNG-WRUNG
絞；擰

不定詞	過去簡單式	過去分詞	意思
STICK	STUCK	STUCK	刺；戳；黏貼；穿
STING	STUNG	STUNG	叮；刺；螫
STINK	STANK	STUNK	發臭
STRIKE	STRUCK	STRUCK	擊；打；攻擊
SWEAR	SWORE	SWORN	發誓；嚴正聲明或承諾
SWEEP	SWEPT	SWEPT	打掃；清除；用掃把清理
SWIM	SWAM	SWUM	游泳
SWING	SWUNG	SWUNG	搖擺；擺動
TAKE	TOOK	TAKEN	拿；取；花費
TEACH	TAUGHT	TAUGHT	教育；教學
TEAR	TORE	TORN	撕開；拉掉；用力拆開
TELL	TOLD	TOLD	告訴；講述；用語言或文字溝通
THINK	THOUGHT	THOUGHT	想；認為
THROW	THREW	THROWN	丟；擲
TREAD	TRODE	TRODDEN	踩踏；步行
UNDERSTAND	UNDERSTOOD	UNDERSTOOD	了解
UPSET	UPSET	UPSET	打亂；使心煩意亂
WAKE UP	WOKE UP	WOKEN UP	醒來；叫醒
WEAR	WORE	WORN	穿；戴
WEAVE	WOVE｜WEAVED	WOVEN｜WEAVED	編；織
WEEP	WEPT	WEPT	哭泣；流淚
WIN	WON	WON	贏
WITHDRAW	WITHDREW	WITHDRAWN	退出；拿回；拿走
WRING	WRUNG	WRUNG	絞；擰
WRITE	WROTE	WRITTEN	寫

lesson

PRESENT CONTINUOUS
[現在進行式]

主詞 + be動詞現在簡單式 + 現在分詞（V-ing）
I'm freezing...
我好冷……

WE ARE CELEBRATING THE CHINESE NEW YEAR. THIS IS THE YEAR OF THE SNAKE.

我們在慶祝中國新年。今年是蛇年。

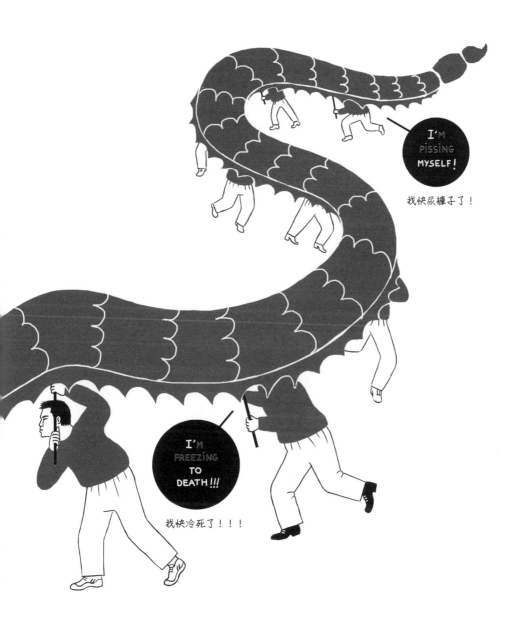

PRESENT CONTINUOUS
NEGATIVE
現在進行式否定句

主詞 + be動詞現在簡單式 + not + 現在分詞（V-ing）
I'm not freezing...
我不冷……

PRESENT CONTINUOUS
QUESTION
現在進行式疑問句

---

be動詞現在簡單式 + 主詞 + 現在分詞（V-ing）
Are you freezing?
你冷嗎？

SiMPLE PRESENT vs. PRESENT CONTINUOUS
[現在簡單式 vs. 現在進行式]

用**現在簡單式**來表示固定發生的動作，或不常改變的事，像是意見。
用**現在進行式**來表示現在發生、暫時的動作，或明確的未來。

THE TEENAGER IS TRYING TO WALK.
那名少年正在努力走路。

THEY ARE HAVING AN AFFAIR.
他們在偷情。

SHE CALLS ME EVERY DAY, BUT TODAY SHE IS NOT CALLING ME.
她每天都打電話給我，但今天沒打來。

I'M A VEGAN. I EAT VEGETABLES. I'M MAKING AN EXCEPTION.
我是個素食者，我吃蔬菜。我現在在破例。

PAST CONTINUOUS
[過去進行式]

主詞＋be動詞過去簡單式＋現在分詞（V-ing）

I was telling...
我那時在講……

I WAS TELLING THE TRUTH WHEN I SAID I WAS AFRAID OF OPEN SPACES.
我說我害怕開放空間時，我是在說實話。

I KNOW.
我知道。

PAST CONTINUOUS
NEGATIVE
過去進行式否定句

主詞 + be動詞過去簡單式 + not + 現在分詞（V-ing）

I was not telling...
我不是在講……

PAST CONTINUOUS
QUESTION
過去進行式疑問句

---

be動詞過去簡單式 + 主詞 + 現在分詞（V-ing）

Was I telling....?
我在講……嗎？

I like apples. Sometimes
they come with a prize.
Yesterday when I was
eating one, a long squirmy
thing appeared from
inside after I took a bite.
It was yummy.

我喜歡蘋果。有時候它
們會帶來獎勵。昨天我
在吃一顆蘋果的時候，
我咬了一口，有一條長
長軟軟的東西從裡面冒
出來。真是好吃。

A prize!
Just like this one.

有獎勵！
就像這一條。

SIMPLE PAST vs. PAST CONTINUOUS
［過去簡單式 vs. 過去進行式］

用**過去簡單式**來表示過去完成的動作。
用**過去進行式**來表示過去特定時刻正在進行的動作。

The tale of the young foreign girl

那個外國小女孩兒的故事

Once upon a time, a young foreign girl <u>was looking</u> for a room in New York City. Nobody <u>wanted</u> her in their apartment. Her problem <u>was</u> that she <u>didn't speak</u> English!

從前從前，有一個外國小女孩兒在紐約市找房子。沒有人想讓她住進他們的公寓。她的問題是她不會說英文！

When the young foreign girl <u>was</u> desperate, after days and weeks of visiting rooms all over the city and talking with potential roommates, she <u>found</u> her chance. One rainy morning she <u>met</u> with a man who <u>was looking</u> for a roommate. It <u>seemed</u> he <u>didn't care</u> about her poor English.

那位外國小女孩兒花了好幾天、甚至好幾週，看遍了市內所有的房間，也和可能的未來室友談過，就在她絕望不已的時候，找到了機會。在一個下雨的早晨，她認識了一個要找室友的男子。看起來他並不在意她的破英文。

They <u>met</u> in the busiest downtown coffee shop. He <u>was</u> quite a lot older than her. He <u>was wearing</u> all black with black-rimmed glasses over a big nose. He <u>looked</u> like an ordinary guy. They both <u>ordered</u> a cup of tea and sat at a small table.

他們在市中心最繁忙的咖啡店碰面。他比她年長很多，穿一身黑，大鼻子上還戴了黑框眼鏡，看起來就像個普通人。他們都點了一杯茶、坐一張小桌旁。

He was very interested in the young girl's life. He didn't stop asking questions. She tried to explain, with her limited knowledge of the language and some gestures, why she was in the city and what she did for a living.

他對那位年輕小女孩兒的人生很感興趣，問題問不停。她試著用她有限的英文知識和一些手勢解釋她為什麼會在這個城市，還有她是做什麼工作的。

Satisfied with her answers, he started to talk about the apartment. It sounded great! Nice place, nice price and friendly roommate. She was grateful for her good luck. Her troubles were over, she thought.

他對她的回答很滿意，然後就開始講公寓的事了。聽起來很棒！不錯的地方、漂亮的價錢和友善的室友。她對自己的好運感到慶幸，心想她的麻煩結束了。

Then the guy showed her some crumpled pictures of a big bright room, a spacious, charming living room, and a clean, tidy kitchen. Meanwhile, he was getting closer to her and he said:

然後那個男子給她看一些皺皺的照片，裡面是一間又大又明亮的房間，有寬敞舒適的客廳，和乾淨整齊的廚房。同時，他也靠她越來越近，他說：

"But there are some conditions. First, you can't have friends over for the first two weeks. Second, you have to be nice to me."

「但是有一些條件。首先，前兩週你不能帶朋友來。再來，你必須對我很好。」

"Well, I'm nice," the young foreigner said. "Why the first condition?"

「嗯，我對人一向很好，」那個外國小女孩兒說：「第一個條件是為什麼呢？」

"Because we will get to know each other faster and it will be easier for us to become friends, close friends," the guy said, smiling. "And there is one more condition. If you are a bad girl, I will beat your young little ass."

「因為這樣我們會較快認識彼此，也比較容易變成朋友，親密的朋友，」那個男子微笑說：「還有一個條件。如果你是個壞女孩，我會打你的小嫩屁喔。」

So the young foreign girl ran away. Even with her limited English, she understood. She is still looking for a room in New York City, visiting apartments and talking with potential roommates... for who knows how long..

所以那個外國小女孩兒就跑掉了。即使英文不好，她還是聽得懂。她還在紐約找房子、看公寓、和可能的未來室友談話……誰知道這會持續多久。

lesson

ADJECTIVES
[形容詞]

TALL
高的

SHORT
矮的

FAT
胖的

SLIM
瘦的

BIG
大的

MEDIUM
中等的

SMALL
小的

形容詞提供與名詞有關的資訊。

形容詞會放在名詞前面：

Thank God, the <u>chatty parrot</u> is sleeping. (~~the parrot chatty~~)
感謝老天爺，那隻喋喋不休的鸚鵡正在睡覺。（鸚鵡的喋喋不休）

不會因為數字而改變：

Blacky is my <u>black cat</u>.
小黑是我的黑貓。
I have eight <u>black cats</u> and I'm still lucky.
我有八隻黑貓，而且我還是很好運。

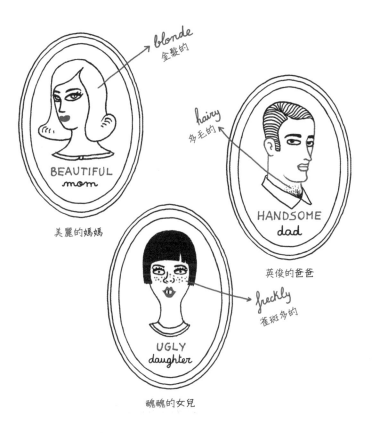

blonde
金髮的

BEAUTIFUL
mom

美麗的媽媽

hairy
多毛的

HANDSOME
dad

英俊的爸爸

UGLY
daughter

醜醜的女兒

freckly
雀斑多的

Life is full of surprises!
人生真是充滿驚奇啊！

POLITE
有禮貌的

DISHONEST 不誠實的

I'm honest

我很誠實。

YOU CAN BE...
你可以是……

ARROGANT	傲慢的
BRAVE	勇敢的
CALM	平靜的
CLEVER	聰明的

GRUMPY
脾氣暴躁的

blah blah
blah
叭啦
blah
blah
blah
叭啦
blah
叭啦

CHATTY
多話的

WISE
有智慧的

DISTRUSTFUL
多疑的

what?
什麼？

WEIRD
奇怪的

CRAZY	瘋狂的	LONELY	孤單的
ENTHUSIASTIC	熱情的	NICE	仁慈的
ENVIOUS	嫉妒的	SARCASTIC	諷刺的
FRIENDLY	友善的	SILLY	傻傻的
FUNNY	有趣的	WITTY	機智的

TOUGH
強悍的

OPTIMISTIC
樂觀的

CHEEKY
厚臉皮的

GOSSIPY
八卦的

JEALOUS
嫉妒的

GIRLY
有少女心的

LAZY
懶惰的

BUT
WICKED
但頑皮的

NUTS
瘋狂的

SHY
害羞的

VAIN
愛慕虛榮的

SELFISH
自私的

SILLY
傻傻的

GLUTTONOUS
貪吃的

PERVERTED
變態的

UPSET - ANGRY
沮喪的一生氣的

SAD
難過的

YOU CAN FEEL...
你可以覺得……

ANXIOUS	焦急的
ASHAMED	感到羞恥的
COOL	涼快的

WARM
溫暖的

HOT
熱的

HAPPY
快樂的

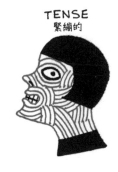

TENSE
緊繃的

DEPRESSED
沮喪的

DISTURBED 感到困擾的

DIZZY   暈眩的

HEALTHY   健康的

ILL   生病的

SLEEPY   想睡覺的

UNEASY   不自在的

WORRIED   擔心的

COLD
寒冷的

HUNGRY
餓的

mmmm!

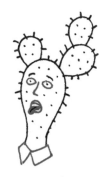

THIRSTY
渴的

PARTICIPIAL ADJECTIVES
[分詞形容詞]

即字尾可以是 ed 和 ing 的形容詞。

字尾為 ed 的形容詞是形容人的感覺。
Laura was <u>bored</u> by the movie.
蘿拉覺得那部電影很無聊。

字尾為 ing 的形容詞是形容人或事給人的感覺。
Laura didn't enjoy the movie because it was <u>boring</u>.
蘿拉並不享受看那部電影，因為那部電影很無聊。

AMAZED 感到驚訝的 AMAZING 令人驚訝的

AMUSED 感覺愉快的 AMUSING 令人覺得有趣的

ANNOYED 感到惱怒的 ANNOYING 讓人氣憤、煩燥的

BORED 覺得無聊的 BORING 無聊的

CONFUSED 困惑的 CONFUSING 令人困惑的

DISAPPOINTED 失望的 DISAPPOINTING 讓人失望的

EXCITED 感到興奮的 EXCITING 令人興奮的

FRIGHTENED 感到害怕的 FRIGHTENING 令人害怕的

INTERESTED 有興趣的 INTERESTING 讓人有興趣的

IRRITATED 惱火的 IRRITATING 令人憤怒的

SURPRISED 感到驚訝的 SURPRISING 令人出奇不意的

THRILLED 刺激興奮的 THRILLING 令人興奮的

ADJECTIVE ORDER
[形容詞的順序]

用一個以上的形容詞時，你得依據類型放對正確的位置。

OPINION 意見

SIZE 大小

AGE 年紀

SHAPE 形狀

冠詞 | 名詞	1 意見	2 大小	3 年紀	4 形狀
a 一個	silly 呆呆的	...	young 年輕	...
the 那個	...	huge 大的	...	round 圓
my 我的	lovely 可愛	...	...	...

COLOR
顏色

ORIGIN
來源

MATERIAL
材料

8
PURPOSE
目的

5 顏色	6 來源	7 材料	8 目的	名詞
...	*Spanish* 西班牙	...	...	*man* 男人
...	...	*wood* 木	...	*bowl* 碗
red 紅色	...	...	*dancing* 舞	*shoes* 鞋

ADJECTIVE + PREPOSITION EXPRESSIONS
[形容詞 + 介系詞的用法]

duck 鴨

We are
FED UP WITH *
crumbs.

We want cheesecake!
We want chocolate!
And we want mint gum!

crumbs
= pieces of bread
麵包屑
= 一小塊一小塊麵包

我們受夠了麵包屑。
我們想吃起士蛋糕!
我們想吃巧克力!
我們也想吃薄荷口香糖!

*再也不能或不願意忍受某種情況。

常見的**形容詞**與常接在後面的**介系詞**：

pacifier
奶嘴

Everyone has a weakness, even those who look strong.
This guy is very **ATTACHED TO*** his pacifier.

每個人都有個弱點，就算是看起來堅強的人也是。這傢伙非常喜歡他的奶嘴。
*喜歡

I'm
HOOKED ON*
coffee.

我有咖啡癮
*成癮

I'm
FASCINATED BY*
science fiction.

我非常喜歡科幻小說。
*非常喜歡

ADDICTED TO 對……著迷
AFRAID OF 害怕……
ANGRY AT 對……生氣
ANXIOUS ABOUT 對……感到焦慮
ASHAMED OF 對……感到羞恥
ATTACHED TO 喜愛……
AWARE OF 知道……
BAD AT 對……不在行
BORED WITH | BY 對……感到無聊
CAPABLE OF 能夠……
CAREFUL OF 小心……
CONCERNED ABOUT 擔心……
CRAZY ABOUT 對……瘋狂
CURIOUS ABOUT 對……好奇
DIFFERENT FROM 與……不同
EXCITED ABOUT 對……感到興奮
FASCINATED BY 著迷於……
FED UP WITH 受夠了……
GLAD ABOUT 對……感到開心
GOOD AT 對……在行
HAPPY ABOUT 對……感到開心
HOOKED ON 沉迷於……
INTERESTED IN 對……有興趣
NERVOUS ABOUT 對……感到緊張
OBSESSED WITH 迷戀於……
PROUD OF 對……感到驕傲
READY FOR 準備好做……
SAFE FROM 免受……的傷害
SATISFIED WITH 對……感到滿意
SICK OF 受不了……
SORRY FOR | ABOUT
對……感到抱歉
TERRIBLE AT 對……不在行
TIRED OF 對……感到疲倦
WORRIED ABOUT 擔心……

COMPARATIVES ［比較級］

YOU ARE OLDER THAN ME.

你比我老。

I'M MORE BEAUTIFUL.

我比較漂亮。

一個音節：	*old* 老的	加 er	*older* 較老的
字尾為子音，前面是母音：	*big* 大的	重複子音，再加 er	*bigger* 較大的
兩個音節：	*careful* 小心的	形容詞前加 more	*more careful* 比較小心的
字尾為y：	*happy* 快樂的	將 y 改成 i，再加er	*happier* 比較快樂的
字尾為er、le、ow：	*narrow* 窄的	加 er	*narrower* 比較窄的
三個音節以上：	*beautiful* 美麗的	形容詞前加 more	*more beautiful* 比較美麗的

SUPERLATIVES
[最高級]

I AM THE BEST
我最優秀。

YOU ARE THE NICEST
你人最好了。

YOU ARE THE MOST HANDSOME
你最帥。

THE CUTEST GUY!
最可愛的男生!

加 est		*oldest* 最老的
重複子音,再加 est		*biggest* 最大的
形容詞前加 most		*most careful* 最小心的
將 y 改成 i,再加 est		*happiest* 最快樂的
加 est		*narrowest* 最窄的
形容詞前加 most		*most beautiful* 最美麗的

例外:

good-better-best
好的—較好的—最好的
bad-worse-worst
壞的—較差的—最差的
far-farther-farthest
遠的—較遠的—最遠的
little-less-least
少的—較少的—最少的
many-more-most
多的—較多的—最多的

AS ... AS
[和······一樣]

"as"用來比較平等的事物：
She is <u>as old as</u> me | I (am).
她跟我年紀一樣大。

也可以用在否定和疑問句：
I'm not <u>as stupid as</u> her | she (is).
我不像她一樣笨。
Is she <u>as beautiful as</u> me | I (am)?
她和我一樣漂亮嗎？

lesson

Adverbs
［副詞］

副詞可修飾動詞、形容詞或另一個動詞。
用來說明某事發生的方式、地點、時間、原因或情況。

She <u>always</u> goes to the café in the <u>afternoon</u> <u>where</u> she has a cup of tea,
<u>probably</u> <u>after</u> spending <u>too</u> <u>much</u> time outside.
她總是在下午去咖啡店，在那邊喝杯茶，可能是在花太多時間待在外面之後。

<u>Surely</u> she is sad.
當然她很難過。

Or <u>maybe</u> <u>simply</u> tired.
或者可能只是疲倦。

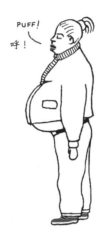

PUFF!

呼！

time adverbs
時間副詞

表示頻率： *sometimes*（有時候）, *frequently*（常常）, *never*（從不）, *often*（通常）, *yearly*（每年）

表示有多久： *all day*（一整天）, *not long*（不久）, *for a while*（一會兒）, *since last year*（自去年起）

表示時間點： *today*（今天）, *yesterday*（昨天）, *later*（稍晚）, *now*（現在）, *last year*（去年）

SHE IS PREGNANT NOW.

她現在有孕在身。

表示時間點的副詞通常放在句尾。

SHE HAS BEEN
PREGNANT FOR NINE MONTHS.

她已經懷孕九個月了。

表示有多久的副詞通常放在句尾。

SHE HAS OFTEN HAD STRANGE
CRAVINGS DURING HER PREGNANCIES.

她在懷孕期間喜歡的東西總是很奇怪。

表示頻率的副詞通常放在主要動詞前、助動詞後面。

表達動作發生確切次數的**頻率**副詞則通常放在句尾。

SHE HAS BEEN PREGNANT FOR NINE MONTHS EVERY YEAR FOR THE LAST DECADE.

她過去十年來，每年都懷孕九個月。

描述時間的副詞一個以上時的順序是：有多久、有多常、時間點。

WHY AM I SO GREAT?
為什麼我這麼了不起?

疑問副詞通常放在問句的最前面。

interrogative adverbs
疑問副詞

why（為什麼）, *where*（在哪裡）, *how*（如何）, *when*（何時）

relative adverbs
關係副詞

where（在哪裡）, *when*（在何時）, *why*（為什麼）

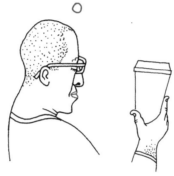

TOM GETS QUITE HORNY
WHEN HE DRINKS COFFEE.

湯姆喝咖啡時都會變得色瞇瞇的。
程度副詞通常放在主要動詞前面，或是放在
修飾的形容詞或副詞前面。

aduerbs of degree
程度副詞

almost（幾乎），*nearly*（幾乎），*just*（就是），*too*（太），*enough*（足夠），
hardly（幾乎不），*completely*（完全），*very*（非常）

地方副詞通常放在主要動詞後面。

她會帶老公出去。

……或放在受詞後面

place adverbs
地方副詞

everywhere（每個地方）, *away*（遠離）, *up*（往上）, *down*（往下）, *around*（周遭）, *out*（往外）, *back*（往回）, *in*（往內）, *outside*（外面）

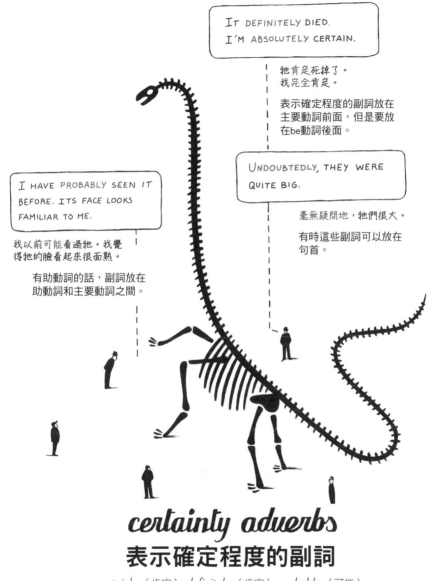

IT DEFINITELY DIED.
I'M ABSOLUTELY CERTAIN.

牠肯定死掉了。
我完全肯定。

表示確定程度的副詞放在
主要動詞前面,但是要放
在be動詞後面。

UNDOUBTEDLY, THEY WERE
QUITE BIG.

毫無疑問地,牠們很大。

有時這些副詞可以放在
句首。

I HAVE PROBABLY SEEN IT
BEFORE. ITS FACE LOOKS
FAMILIAR TO ME.

我以前可能看過牠。我覺
得牠的臉看起來很面熟。

有助動詞的話,副詞放在
助動詞和主要動詞之間。

certainty adverbs
表示確定程度的副詞

certainly(肯定), *definitely*(肯定), *probably*(可能),
undoubtedly(毫無疑問地), *surely*(肯定)

manner adverbs
狀態副詞

well（良好）, *rapidly*（快速地）, *slowly*（緩慢地）, *quickly*（迅速地）,
easily（容易地）, *loudly*（大聲地）, *softly*（柔軟地）, *beautifully*（美麗地）

SHE SPENDS HER SALARY QUICKLY.
SHE SPENDS IT EASILY.

SHE HAPPILY BETS AGAINST THE MACHINE.

她薪水花得很快，花錢如流水。
狀態副詞通常放在主要動詞或受詞後面。

她開心地跟機器對賭。
如果動詞為及物動詞，狀態副詞可以放在
動詞前面做為強調。

I THINK SHE IS CERTAINLY THE WORST PERSON I HAVE EVER KNOWN. DON'T YOU THINK?

找覺得她肯定是我所認識最糟糕的人了，你不覺得嗎？

評論副詞和意見副詞很類似，但它們是放在be動詞後面，和主要動詞前面。

FRANKLY, MY DEAR, I DON'T GIVE A DAMN.

坦白說，親愛的，找根本不在乎。

意見副詞放在句首，用逗號將句子其他部分區隔開來。

viewpoint adverbs
意見副詞

honestly（老實說）, *frankly*（坦白說）, *personally*（個人來講）,
obviously（顯然）, *surely*（肯定）, *undoubtedly*（無疑地）

and commenting adverbs
和評論副詞

definitely（絕對）, *certainly*（肯定）, *obviously*（顯然）, *simply*（單純地）

iN, ON, AT
place prepositions
[地方介系詞 IN、ON、AT]

IN 在……裡面
在一個區域或空間裡面

in the city 在城市
in New York 在紐約
in bed 在床上
in my pocket 在我的口袋裡
in the car 在車裡

ON 在……上面
與某個表面接觸

on the table 在桌上
on the wall 在牆上
on the floor 在地上
on the carpet 在地毯上
on the door 在門上

AT 在……
指位置

at the corner 在角落
at the end of the street 在街尾
at the entrance 在入口
at the station 在車站
at the top of the page 在頁首

談交通方式時：
in a | the: *car, truck* 在汽車、卡車裡
on a | the: *subway, bus, train, airplane, ship, bicycle*
在地鐵、公車、火車、飛機、船、腳踏車上

常見用法：
in: *in a car, in a taxi, in an elevator, in the newspaper, in the sky, in Times Square*
在汽車裡、在計程車裡、在電梯裡、在報紙上、在天空中、在時代廣場
on: *on a bus, on a train, on an airplane, on the radio, on the Internet, on the left*
在公車上、在火車上、在飛機上、在收音機裡、在網路上、在左邊
at: *at home, at work, at school, at college, at the bottom, at the reception*
在家、在公司、在學校、在大學裡、在底部、在接待處

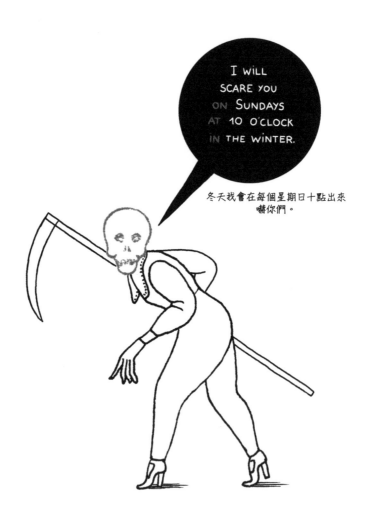

iN, ON, AT

time prepositions

[時間介系詞 IN、ON、AT]

IN 在……

月份、季節, 年份、世紀

in April 在四月
in summer 在夏天
in 1900 | in the 1900s
在一九〇〇年、在一九〇〇年代
in the past century
在過去那一世紀中
in the future 在未來

ON 在……

日子和日期

on Sunday 在週日
on Mondays 在每週一
on September the 4th
在九月四日
on his birthday 在他的生日
on New Year's Eve 在除夕夜

AT 在……

時間整點、時間點

at 5 o'clock 在五點
at noon | night 在中午、在晚上
at bedtime 在就寢時間
at the moment 在那時候
at the end of the week 在週末

常見用法：

in: *in the morning(s), in the afternoon(s), in the evening(s)* 在早上、在下午、在晚上
on: *on Tuesday morning(s), on Wednesday afternoon(s), on weekends*
在週二早上、在週三下午、在週末
at: *at night, at Christmas, at the same time* 在晚上、在聖誕節、在同一個時間

用 last、next、every 或 this 時，不可加 in、on 或 at：

I was depressed last May. (not ~~in last May~~) 我去年五月時很沮喪。
I'm planning to rob a bank next Monday. (not ~~on next Monday~~) 我打算下週一去搶一間銀行。
I eat donuts every Christmas. (not ~~at every Christmas~~) 我每年聖誕節都會吃甜甜圈。
I will take a walk naked this evening. (not ~~in this evening~~) 今晚我會裸體去散步。

lesson

TiCK TOCK

• WHAT TIME IS IT? •
［滴答滴答］
現在幾點鐘？

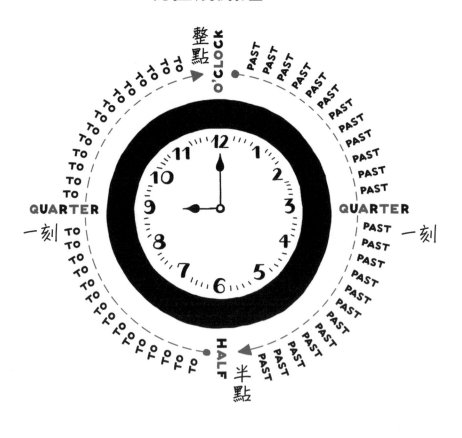

TWENTY PAST EIGHT
八點二十分

A QUARTER PAST SEVEN
七點一刻
（7：15）

A QUARTER TO TWO
差十五分就兩點了
（1：45）

HALF PAST TWELVE
OR
TWELVE THIRTY
十二點半或十二點三十分
（12：30）

SIX O'CLOCK
六點鐘
（6：00）

FIVE TO FOUR
差五分就四點了
（4：55）

Helena is waiting for her lover.
They had a date at _a quarter to eight_.
She is still waiting for him.
海蓮娜在等她的情人。
他們約的時間是七點四十五分。
她還在等他。

Claudine arranged a date with the guy who has
been giving her flowers for the last two months.
The date was at _seven o'clock_. She won't be getting any more flowers.
克蘿汀跟一個上個月一直送她花的男子安排了約會。
約會時間是在七點整。她不會再收到任何花了。

The guy who Jennifer is waiting for should have arrived at a <u>quarter past eight</u>. He is fifteen minutes late so far. Perhaps she will be luckier than the other two girls.
珍妮佛一直在等的男子應該在八點十五分
到。他目前已經遲到十五分鐘了。或許她會
比其他兩個女孩兒幸運。

Waiting in a café
在咖啡廳裡等待著

★ during the day ★
一天之中

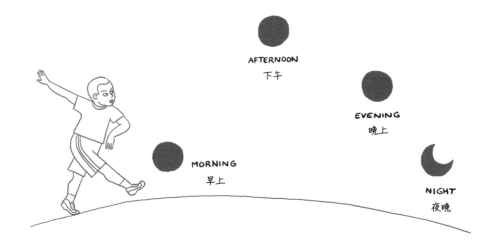

AFTERNOON
下午

EVENING
晚上

MORNING
早上

NIGHT
夜晚

招呼語：
GOOD MORNING 早安：從你起床到中午十二點。
GOOD AFTERNOON 午安：從中午十二點（或午餐過後）到下午五點。
GOOD EVENING 晚上好：下午五點過後。
GOOD NIGHT 晚安：晚上時間或睡覺前的道別。

---

12 p.m. = 下午十二點 = 中午或正午 | 12 a.m.= 上午十二點 = 午夜
11 a.m.（上午十一點）後，是 12 p.m.（下午十二點），
所以 11 p.m.（下午十一點）後，就是 12 a.m.（上午十二點）
A.M.（上午）意思是 *ante meridiem*（中午之前）。
P.M.（下午）意思是 *post meridiem*（中午之後）。

DAYS OF THE WEEK：一週之中

一週之中每一天的首字母都要大寫。

Sunday	星期日
Monday	星期一
Tuesday	星期二
Wednesday	星期三
Thursday	星期四
Friday	星期五
Saturday	星期六

SABBATH!
安息日

（編按：對猶太人及少數基督教徒來說是星期六，對一般基督教徒而言是星期日。）

—MONTHS—
[月份]

1 JANUARY 一月
2 FEBRUARY 二月
3 MARCH 三月
4 APRIL 四月
5 MAY 五月
6 JUNE 六月
7 JULY 七月
8 AUGUST 八月
9 SEPTEMBER 九月
10 OCTOBER 十月
11 NOVEMBER 十一月
12 DECEMBER 十二月

THE 4 SEASONS
[四季]

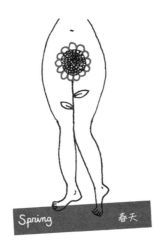

Spring　春天

Summer　夏天

Fall　秋天

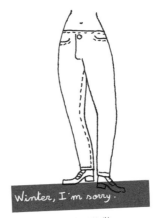

Winter, I'm sorry.

冬天，我很抱歉。

WHAT'S THE DATE?
[今天幾號？]

英文日期的寫法
dates in written English

September 4, 2007

4th September, 2007 → Br. English　（英式英文）

September 4th, 2007 → Am. English　（美式英文）

9/4/07

二〇〇七年九月四日

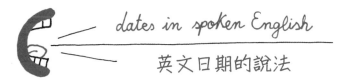
dates in spoken English

英文日期的說法

September fourth, two thousand and seven.

September the fourth, two thousand and seven.

The fourth of September, two thousand and seven.

二〇〇七年九月四日

lesson

10

THE FUTURE is WILL [未來式 WILL]

主詞 + will + 原型動詞
I will love... 我會愛……

未來式 **will** 用來表達關於未來的
預測和事實。

> I will have seven children.
> I will get married to a rich
> and handsome man. My
> wonderful husband will love me
> very much. He will sow seven
> seeds in me, from which seven
> children will grow. Seven is
> my lucky number. Blue is my
> favorite color. But what I
> like most is pizza.

我將會有七個小孩。我會嫁給一個多金帥哥。我那美好的老公將會非常愛我。他會在
我身體裡種下七顆種子,這七顆種子會長大變成我的七個小孩。七是我的幸運數字。
藍色是我最喜歡的顏色。但我最喜歡的是披薩。

will 也會用在:

做出臨場反應。
The telephone is ringing. I <u>will answer</u> it!
電話響了。我來接!

表示想要做或願意做。
I hope you <u>will come</u> to my apartment tonight.
我希望今晚你願意來我家。

表示提議或承諾。
I <u>will bring</u> some food. 我會帶些食物。
She always says she <u>will cook</u>, but she is a disaster when it comes to cooking.
她老是說要做飯,可是說到做飯,她可是一點兒也不行。

FUTURE WILL *question*

未來式 will 的問句

will + 主詞 + 原型動詞

Will you be....? 你將會……嗎？

未來式 will 的否定句

主詞 + will not | won't + 原型動詞

I won't grow up! 我不要長大

FUTURE WILL *negative*

the other future:
be going to
[其他的未來式：be going to]

主詞 + be動詞 + going to + 原型動詞
I'm going to dance... 我要跳舞……

未來式 be going to 用來形容
未來的計畫和意圖。

I'M GOING TO LEAVE MY JOB.

我要離職。

I'M GOING TO GIVE AWAY MY STUFF.

我要把我的東西送走。

I'M GOING TO DANCE EVERY NIGHT.

我要每晚都跳舞。

I'M GOING TO GO TO THE CONGO.

我要去剛果。

她的美夢不會成真的。

未來式be going to也用來表達根據當下證據所做的**預測**。

*She is going to stay the same and
forget about all her plans.*
她仍會是老樣子，忘光她所做的計畫。

口語中 going to = gonna

否定句

主詞 + be動詞 + not + going + 不定詞
She's not going to accomplish her plans. 她不會完成她的計畫。

疑問句

主詞 + be動詞 + not + going + 不定詞
Is she going to stop complaining? 她要停止抱怨了嗎？

★ **FUTURE** CONTINUOUS ★
[未來進行式]

主詞 + will be + 現在分詞（V-ing）
I will be waiting...
我會等著……

未來進行式用在：
一個動作將會在未來持續進行。
She'll be waiting until her husband arrives.
她將會一直等到她先生來。

我會不睡覺等你。

我大約晚上
十點會到。

未來某個特定時間會發生的動作。
Next year they will be enjoying their mornings just as much.
明年他們還是會一樣享受著他們的早晨時光。

正式的提議。

Will you <u>be eating</u> some appetizers, madam?
小姐，你要用一些開胃菜嗎？
Yes, I will. Mmm... delicious!
好，我要。嗯……好吃！

小姐，你要用一些開胃菜嗎？

確認資訊。

Will you <u>be having</u> lunch with us?
你會跟我們一起吃中飯嗎？
Sure! <u>Will</u> you <u>be going</u> to the party later?
當然！你等一下會去派對嗎？

你會跟我們一起吃中飯嗎？

對人們的感覺做同理預測。

You'll be needing to unwind after a hard day of work.
在辛苦工作一天之後，你會需要放鬆一下。
I'm going to be needing a blossom tea.
我會需要一杯花茶。

在辛苦工作一天之後，你會需要放鬆一下。

★ FUTURE CONTINUOUS ★
negatives
未來進行式的否定句

主詞 + will not be | won't be + 現在分詞（V-ing）
She won't be waiting... 她不會一直等著……

或者用 **be going to**
主詞 + is | are + not + going to be + 現在分詞（V-ing）
She's not going to be waiting... 她不會一直等著……

I WON'T BE WAITING FOR YOU.

我不會一直等著你。

★ FUTURE CONTINUOUS ★
questions
未來進行式的疑問句

Will + 主詞 + **be** + 現在分詞（**V-ing**）
Will you be needing...? 你會需要⋯⋯嗎？

或用**be going to**
be 動詞 + 主詞 + **going to be** + 現在分詞（**V-ing**）
Are you going to be needing...? 你會需要⋯⋯嗎？

你會需要放鬆一下嗎？

lesson 11

simple PRESENT PERFECT
［現在完成式］

I have been happily married <u>since</u> I met this man.

主詞 + have | has + 過去分詞
I have spent... 我已經花了⋯⋯

I have spent my parents' savings.

自從我認識了這個男人之後就一直是個幸福人妻。

我已經花掉了父母的存款。

how long（有多久）、for（有）、since（自從）用在一般不能用在進行式的動詞；be、have、know、like。

用在未指定時間但**已完成的**動作。

I have not <u>ever</u> been to Miami.

I have had <u>six</u> beers.

這是我一生中感覺最棒的時刻。

It's the <u>best</u> feeling I've <u>ever</u> had in my whole life.

我從來沒去過邁阿密。

我喝了六杯啤酒。

用在有ever（曾經）、already（已經）、yet（還沒）、just（剛剛）的時候。

用在我們說出how many（有多少）或how many times（有幾次）的時候。

用在有**最高級**的時候。

PRESENT PERFECT *continuous*
［現在完成進行式］

主詞 + have | has + been + 現在分詞
（V-ing）
I have been cheating. 我一直在偷吃……

I have been spending time with Susan today.

自從我老婆開始打呼後，我就一直在偷吃。

我今天一直跟蘇珊在一起消磨時光。

NO SMOKING

I have been cheating on my wife since she started snoring.

用在持續的動作，特別是有how long（有多久）的問題以及有for（有）、since（自從）的回答。

用在最近剛完成的**持續動作**。

simple PRESENT PERFECT
[現在完成式]

negative 否定

主詞 + **haven't** | **hasn't** + 過去分詞

I haven't forgotten... 我沒忘了……

question 疑問

have | **has** + 主詞 + 過去分詞

Have you lost...? 你失去了……嗎？

Present Perfect continuous
［現在完成進行式］

小乖乖，你一直在吃巧克力嗎？

HAVE YOU BEEN EATING CHOCOLATE, HONEY?

NO, I HAVEN'T BEEN EATING ANYTHING, MOMMY.

沒有，我一直沒有吃東西，媽咪。

negative 否定

主詞 + haven't | hasn't + been + 現在分詞（V-ing）

I haven't been eating... 我一直沒有吃⋯⋯

question 疑問

have | has + 主詞 + been + 現在分詞（V-ing）

Have you been eating? 你一直在吃東西嗎？

PRESENT PERFECT or SIMPLE PAST ?
[現在完成式還是過去簡單式？]

I always thought dinosaurs were just science fiction.

81ST ST. MUSEUM OF NATURAL HISTORY.

→ 81 →

I have believed in the existence of dinosaurs since I met you.

我一直以為恐龍只是科幻小說。

自從我認識了你之後，我就相信恐龍的存在了。

過去簡單式通常用在已完成的動作，並且有表達過去時間的字詞 yesterday（昨天）、ago（以前）、last week（上週）……

I always <u>thought</u> dinosaurs were just science fiction.
我一直以為恐龍只是科幻小說。
= she doesn't think so anymore. 她不再這麼認為。

現在完成式通常用在動作是過去開始的，而且現在還在進行中。

<u>*I have believed*</u> *in the existence of dinosaurs since I met you.*
自從我認識了你之後，我就相信恐龍的存在了。
= he still believes they exist.
他仍相信牠們存在。

simple PAST PERFECT
［過去完成式］

主詞 + had + 過去分詞
I had fallen... 我跌落了……

講的是發生在過去另一個事件之前的行動。

通常會用描述時間的副詞，如：
already（已經）、just（剛剛）、never（未曾）、ever（曾經）、before（以前）

She had never fallen off her bike before the time when she broke her leg.
在她摔斷腿前，過去騎腳踏車沒從摔車過。

> I HAD NEVER FALLEN OFF MY BIKE BEFORE.

我過去騎腳踏車從沒摔車過。

> SHE TOLD ME THAT HE HAD TOLD HER THAT ELISA IS PREGNANT.

她告訴我他跟她說艾莉莎懷孕了。

也可以用在**轉述句**。
She whispered what they had said.
她小小聲說了他們說的事。

> OH MY GOD!

哦，我的老天爺！

PAST PERFECT *continuous*
[過去完成進行式]

主詞 + had been + 現在分詞（V-ing）
She had been dancing... 她那時一直在跳舞……

講的是過去開始發生的**行動**，然後**持續到另一個過去的事件**發生為止。

She <u>had been dancing</u> until her back said "stop".
她那時一直在跳舞，直到她的背說「別跳了」。

simple PAST PERFECT
[過去完成式]

HAD YOU EVER BEEN ANYWHERE THAT HAD SO MANY PEOPLE BEFORE YOU CAME TO THE CITY？

你來到這個城市之前去過任何一個有這麼多人的地方嗎？

NO, I HADN'T. AND I HADN'T EVER FELT THIS ALONE, EITHER.

不，沒有過。而且我也未曾感到如此孤單。

negative 否定

主詞 + hadn't + 過去分詞
I hadn't felt... 我那時並未感到……

question 疑問

had + 主詞 + 過去分詞
Had you been...? 你過去一直……嗎？

PAST PERFECT *continuous*
［過去完成進行式］

> HAD YOU BEEN STEALING FROM YOUR CLIENTS BEFORE THE COMPANY WENT BANKRUPT?

在公司破產前，你有一直在偷拿客戶的東西嗎？

> NO, I HADN'T BEEN STEALING. I HAD BEEN INVESTING IN MYSELF.

不，我並沒有一直偷拿。我一直在投資我自己。

negative 否定

主詞 + hadn't + been + 現在分詞（V-ing）

I hadn't been stealing... 我並沒有一直偷……

question 疑問

had + 主詞 + been + 現在分詞（V-ing）

Had you been stealing? 你一直在偷東西嗎？

simple FUTURE PERFECT
[未來完成式]

主詞 + will have + 過去分詞
I will have succeeded... 我會成功了……

用來表示一個動作在未來某個時間點將會完成。

He *will have succeeded* in making a friend by the time he's no longer afraid of people.
一直到他不再害怕人群時，就會成功交到朋友了。

When he makes a friend,
he *will have overcome* his fear of people.
當他交到朋友時，就會克服對人群的恐懼了。

BY NEXT SPRING, MAYBE I'LL HAVE SUCCEEDED IN MAKING A FRIEND.

到了下個春天，或許我就會成功交到一個朋友了。

FUTURE PERFECT *continuous*
[未來完成進行式]

主詞 + will have been + 現在分詞（V-ing）
I will have been working... 我將已經工作了……

I'LL HAVE BEEN WORKING FOR 16 HOURS WHEN I FINISH MY SHIFT.

等我輪完班時，我就已經工作十六個小時了。

用來表示一個行動在未來的**另一個動作發生之前**會進行多久。
She will have been working for 16 hours and she will still have to prepare dinner for her husband.
她到時候就已經工作十六個小時了，而且她仍將得替老公準備晚餐。

simple FUTURE PERFECT
[未來完成式]

下一次萬聖節時，我會不
會已經重拾自信了呢？

我不知道。不過我知道
你那時還不會原諒你媽。

negative 否定

主詞 + won't have + 過去分詞
You won't have forgiven... 你不會已經原諒……

question 疑問

will + 主詞 + have + 過去分詞
Will I have gotten...? 我會已經得到了……嗎？

FUTURE PERFECT continuous
［未來完成進行式］

HOW LONG WILL I HAVE BEEN TRYING TO LEARN ENGLISH AFTER THIS? 3, 4 YEARS... 6 YEARS... OH WELL, I WON'T HAVE BEEN WASTING MY TIME IF I FINALLY DO LEARN.

在此之後，我會試著學英文多久了呢？三、四年……六年……哦，嗯，如果我最後學會了，就不算是一直浪費時間了。

negative 否定

主詞 + won't have been + 現在分詞（V-ing）
I won't have been wasting... 我就不會一直浪費了……

question 疑問

will + 主詞 + have been + 現在分詞（V-ing）
Will I have been trying...? 我會已經試了……嗎？

[所有的動詞時態]

現在時態	過去	現在	未來
現在簡單式		*I want cookies.* 我想要餅乾。	*The movie starts at 5 p.m.* 電影下午五點開始。
		I am silly. 我傻傻的。	
現在進行式		*I'm driving right now.* 我現在正在開車。	*I'm meeting friends tonight.* 我今晚要和朋友碰面。
		I'm living in New York. 我現在住在紐約。	
現在完成式	*I have been to Italy.* 我去過義大利。	*I have cleaned the room.* 我打掃好房間了。	
現在完成進行式	*I have been drinking.* 我一直有在喝酒。		
		I have been waiting in line for 2 hours. 我已經排隊等了兩個小時了。	

過去時態

	過去	現在	未來
過去簡單式	*I played with dolls.* 我跟娃娃玩。	*If I lied to you, you would know!* 如果我對你說謊，你會知道。	*If you forgot to bring it, I'd remind you.* 如果你忘了帶這個，我會提醒你。
過去進行式	*I was sleeping at 11 a.m.* 早上十一點的時候，我還在睡覺。		*If I wasn't working tomorrow, I would go.* 如果我明天不用上班，我會去。
過去完成式	*I had lost some weight.* 我的體重已經輕一點了。		
過去完成進行式	*I had been crying all day.* 我一整天都在哭。	*If I had been reading, I wouldn't have seen you.* 如果我一直在讀書，就不會見到你了。	

未來時態

	過去	現在	未來
未來式		*I'll answer the phone.* 我會接電話。	*I will buy the tickets tomorrow.* 我明天會買票。
未來進行式			*I will be having dinner with friends.* 我會和朋友吃晚餐。
未來完成式			*I will have finished.* 我會完成了。
	I will have lived here for five years next week. 下週我就住在這裡五年了。		
未來完成進行式			*I'll have been waiting for 2 hours when you arrive.* 你到的時候，我就已經等兩個小時了。
	Soon, I will have been driving for 12 hours. 很快地，我就要開車開十二個小時了。		

lesson

12

[動名詞還是不定詞？]

動名詞

用在**介系詞**後面。
I'm tired of <u>running</u>. 我跑不動了。

用在**某些動詞**之後：
like（喜歡）, love（愛）, hate（討厭；恨）, enjoy（享受）, mind（介意）, finish（完成）, stop（停止）.
I enjoy <u>seeing</u> you. 我喜歡見到你。

當作句子的**主詞**。
<u>*Smoking*</u> *is a pleasure.* 抽菸是件樂事。

不定詞

用在**形容詞**後面。
This problem is difficult <u>to solve</u>.
這個問題很難解決。

用在**某些動詞**之後：
would like（想要）, want（想要）, need（需要）, decide（決定）, hope（希望）, expect（預期）, plan（計畫）, forget（忘記）, seem（似乎）, try（試圖）, promise（承諾）, offer（提供）, refuse（拒絕）, learn（學習）, manage（努力完成）.
I would like <u>to escape</u>. 我想要逃跑。

表達目的、原因。
I'm chasing this guy <u>to earn</u> my bread and butter. 我在追求這個人，賺我的飯票。

這是個很難解決的情況。
我喜歡看你很累的樣子，
但我也想逃跑。

停下來！我跑不動了。

• USUALLY •
• USED TO •
• BE USED TO •
• GET USED TO •
[通常、以前總是、習慣、習慣]

USUALLY 通常

用在目前的習慣。

主詞 + **usually** + 動詞

Melissa, a good English teacher, usually makes students repeat sentences correctly.
梅莉莎是一名優秀的英文老師,通常會要學生正確地複誦句子。
This usually bothers Meritxell, her student, a little. 這通常會讓她的學生梅莉瑟兒有點困擾。

USED TO 以前總是

用在過去的習慣,或是已改變的過去情況。

主詞 + **used to** + 原型動詞

Meritxell used to take drugs, but now she doesn't even smoke.
梅莉瑟兒以前會吸毒,不過現在連菸都不抽了。

BE USED TO 習慣

用在你已經適應的新情況。

主詞 + **be used to** + 動名詞或名詞

Melissa is used to craving food all the time since she quit smoking.
梅莉莎自從戒菸後就習慣一直吃東西。

GET USED TO 習慣

用在你越來越熟悉的事物,或你正在適應中的事物。

主詞 + **get used to** +動名詞或名詞

Melissa and Meritxell haven't gotten used to living without addictions.
梅莉莎和梅莉瑟兒還沒習慣過沒有癮頭的日子。

[希望]
WISHES

我希望你在這兒。

I WISH YOU WERE HERE.

I WISH WE WERE LYING IN BED TOGETHER.

我希望我們一起躺在床上。

NY IS COLD

wish常用來表達遺憾，或是不真實的情況。
用於**現在**和**未來**的希望：

用**過去簡單式**來表達你希望情況有所不同。
He wishes she were here.
他希望她在這裡。

用**過去進行式**來表達你想要做不同的事。
He wishes they were lying on the bed.
他希望他們躺在床上。

I、he、she、it 都是用 were。

現在我希望你沒有過來。

Now I wish you hadn't come over.

I wish you would stop laughing at me.

我希望你不要再笑我了。

ha ha ha ha

用於**過去**的希望：

用**過去完成式**表示遺憾，
或你希望情況有所不同。
He _wishes_ she _hadn't come_ over.
他希望她沒有過來。

用來抱怨，或表達不耐煩：

用 would + 動詞
He _wishes_ she _would stop_ laughing.
他希望她不要再笑了。

或用 could + 動詞
He _wishes_ he _could make_ her disappear.
他希望他能讓她消失。

在慣用語中，可以用**主詞 + wish + 代名詞**：_I wish you_ the best. 我真心祝福你。

[寧願]
RATHER
at The Museum of Modern Art
在當代美術館

多看看,學著點!你
得當個另類藝術家。

噢,老爸!我寧願當
個服務生就好。

RATHER 寧願

用來表達喜好。

RATHER THAN

意思是「不要」或「不是」。
通常用來比較平行的結構。

> HE IS A SEX MANIAC RATHER THAN
> AN ART ENTHUSIAST.

他是個性愛狂，而不是個藝術狂。

WOULD RATHER... THAN

表示「寧願做……」，
用來在選項間表明喜好。
主詞 + would rather + 原型動詞 + 選項一
+ than + 選項二

> ELVIS WOULD RATHER
> BE THE CENTER OF ATTENTION
> THAN
> BE JUST LIKE EVERYBODY ELSE.

艾維斯喜歡成為注意焦點，而不只是像其他
每個人一樣。

WOULD RATHER

意思是「寧願」。
用來表明喜歡某一個選項，勝過另一個。
主詞 + would rather + 原型動詞 + 選項

> – HEY JEFF! LET'S GET OUT OF HERE!
> –I'D RATHER STAY HERE.

一嘿，傑夫！我們離開這裡吧。
一我想要留在這裡。

OR RATHER（應該說是）

用來改變剛剛說的。

> SHE IS DISTRACTED, OR RATHER, SHE
> IS PRETENDING TO BE DISTRACTED.

她不專心，或者應該說，她假裝不專心。

RATHER（頗為）

也是一個程度副詞，意思是「相當」。

> MARILYN HAD A RATHER TENDER LOOK.

瑪莉蓮看起來滿溫柔的。

CONNECTORS
[連接詞]

連接詞用來表示想法之間的關係。

> The last clue drove Harry to the wood house on top of the mountain. Maybe this would be the telltale clue. The weather was very bad and, in addition, the car lights didn't work because they had been shot out a couple of hours earlier. Despite all this, Harry managed to get to the place and get out of the car unnoticed. The lights of the house were on so Harry carefully crawled through the bushes until he reached the window. There he saw Elisabeth crying. Suddenly, a shiver came over his body. Instead of crying, Elisabeth was actually laughing and looking directly into Harry's eyes while holding the gun.

最後一個線索讓哈利跑到山頂那棟木屋了。或許這會是洩露內情的線索。天氣非常糟，而且，車燈壞了，因為車燈在幾小時之前被射壞了。儘管這一切種種，哈利還是成功到了那個地方，然後走出車子而沒有被看到。房子的燈亮著，所以哈利小心地爬過灌木叢，爬到窗戶邊。他在那邊看到伊莉莎白在哭，突然間，他身體一陣哆嗦。伊莉莎白不是在哭，她其實是在笑，而且手拿著槍，同時直楞楞地看著哈利的眼睛。

連接詞的類型，按意思來分類：

舉例
for example (e.g.)（比如）, *for instance*（舉例來說）, *such as*（例如）

引入主題
with regard to, regarding, concerning（以上均為「關於」）, *by the way*（順道一提）

加入資訊
and（而且）, *also*（也）, *too*（也）, *as well as*（而且）, *in addition*（另外）, *apart from*（此外）, *besides*（除了）, *furthermore*（再者）, *moreover*（而且）, *then again*（另一方面）

做摘要
in short（簡單來說）, *in brief*（簡言之）, *in summary*（簡言之）, *to conclude*（做為總結）, *in conclusion*（結論是）

提供理由
because, because of, for, since, as, due to（以上均為「因為」）, *owing to*（由於）

引入發展
so, consequently, as a result, therefore, thus, hence（以上均為「因此」「所以」）

表現對比
but（但是）, *however*（然而）, *although, even though, though*（以上均為「雖然」）, *despite, in spite of, nevertheless*（以上均為「儘管」）, *nonetheless*（仍然）, *while*（然而）, *whereas*（然而）, *unlike*（不同於）, *on the other hand*（另一方面）, *anyway*（無論如何）

想法排序
firstly（首先）, *secondly*（第二）, *thirdly*（第三）, *to begin with*（首先）, *next*（接著）, *lastly*（最後）, *finally*（最後）

陳述中使用
at the beginning（首先）, *then*（然後）, *at last*（最後）, *once*（曾經）, *afterwards*（後來）, *suddenly*（突然）, *finally*（最後）, *in the end*（最後）

強調
obviously（顯然）, *particularly*（特別是）, *in theory*（理論上）, *in fact*（事實上）, *especially*（特別是）

表示肯定
surely（當然）, *indeed*（的確）, *undoubtedly*（無疑）, *certainly*（肯定）, *even so*（儘管如此）

Relative Clauses
［關係子句］

關係子句是一個獨立的子句，可修飾一個字、一組字詞，
或是主要子句裡的概念。
關係子句的開頭是**關係代名詞**：

who（誰）、whom（誰）、whose（誰的）、that（那個）或which（哪個）。
（在某些情況中，what、when 和 where 可以作關係代名詞用。）

子句的種類會決定要用哪個關係代名詞。

有兩種關係子句：

非限定子句和限定子句。

NEWS

35   OCTOBER 1, 2007

The press, which is threatened by rapidly changing technology, is making a daily effort to keep its readers' interest or, rather, lack thereof.
Our newspaper has gotten in on the act too!

新聞

媒體被快速變遷的科技威脅著，每天都努力吸引讀者的興趣，或者這麼說吧，讓讀者因此興趣缺缺。敝報也已加入了這個行列！

那個一邊慢跑一邊推著嬰兒
推車的女人是我的英雄。

Defining Clauses
限定子句

限定子句內含的資訊是**很重要的**。
如果刪掉，所談論的人或事物
就不清楚了。

在這類子句中，關係代名詞：
講人用who、that
（介系詞後用的則是whom）
講事物用which、that。

這種子句**不能用逗號分開**。

*The woman <u>who is pushing a stroller</u>
is her heroine.*
那個推著嬰兒推車的女人是她的英雄。

那我呢？

運動，應該是有益健康的，
卻讓找快死了。

Non-Defining Clauses
非限定子句

非限定子句內含的資訊不是**很重要**。
如果刪掉，所談論的人或事物
還是很清楚。

在這類子句中，關係代名詞：
講人用who（whom和whose）
講事物用which（whose）。

這種子句要用**逗號**和主要子句分開。

Exercise, <u>which is supposed to be good for your health</u>, is killing her.
運動，應該是有益健康的，卻讓她快死了。

ACTIVE & PASSIVE VOICES
[主動語態和被動語態]

英文中有兩種語態：主動語態和被動語態。

主動語態描述主詞所做的事。
The dog bit Julianne's leg. 那隻狗咬了茱莉安的腿。

被動語態描述主詞的遭遇。
通常用在我們不知道執行這個動作的人是誰或對是誰沒有興趣。
Julianne's leg was bitten by some dog.
茱莉安的腿被某隻狗咬了。

被動語態的結構是：

be動詞 + 過去分詞
is made... 被做⋯⋯

也可以寫作：
to get + **過去分詞**
got broken... 被打破⋯⋯

所有動詞時態都能用被動語態來表達。
The concert <u>will be performed</u> next week. 演奏會將於下週表演。
The concert <u>has been performed</u> already. 演奏會已經演出過了。

by 用來顯示做這個動作的人或事物。
The painting was made <u>by</u> a monkey.
這幅畫是由一隻猴子畫的。

THE PIGEONS ARE EATING A WORM.
鴿子在吃一隻蟲。

WORMS ARE EATEN EVERY DAY
ALL OVER THE WORLD.
世界各地每天都有蟲子被吃掉。

Reported Speech
[轉述句]

I NEED A FRIEND ASAP.

SHE SAID SHE NEEDED A FRIEND ASAP.

她說她需要盡快有個朋友。

我需要盡快有個朋友。

有兩種方式重述其他人說的話：

直述句和轉述句。

直述句用引號和原文來表達。
She said "I need a friend". 她說：「我需要一個朋友。」

轉述句則是間接的。
She said she needed a friend. 她說她需要一個朋友。

轉述句是用直述句的過去式。
"I <u>need</u> a friend."「我需要一個朋友。」 - *She said she <u>needed</u> a friend.* 她說她需要一個朋友。
"I<u>'m feeling</u> alone."「我覺得孤單。」 - *She said she <u>was feeling</u> alone.* 她說她覺得孤單。
"I<u>'ve spent</u> all Sunday watching TV."「我星期天一整天都在看電視。」
- *She said she <u>had spent</u> all Sunday watching TV.* 她說她星期天一整天都在看電視。
"I <u>will go</u> to bed early."「我要早點睡覺。」
- *She said she <u>would go</u> to bed early.* 她說她要早點睡覺。

當直述句用的是過去式時，轉述句則不用改。
"I <u>was</u> afraid."「我很害怕。」 - *She said she <u>was</u> afraid.* 她說她很害怕。
"I <u>was looking</u> for a better life."「我在尋找更美好的生活。」
- *She said she <u>was looking</u> for a better life.* 她說她在尋找更美好的生活。

lesson

PHRASAL VERBS

[片語動詞]

片語動詞是慣用語，結合了**動詞**和**介系詞**或**副詞**而形成新的動詞。

FACE UP TO

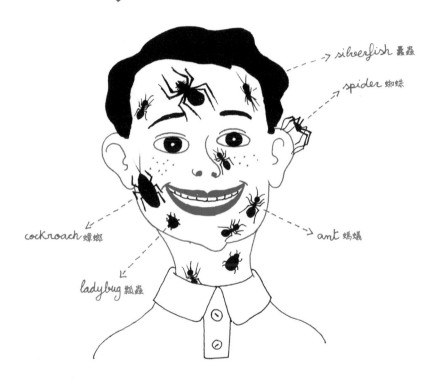

→ silverfish 蠹蟲
→ spider 蜘蛛
cockroach 蟑螂 ←
→ ant 螞蟻
ladybug 瓢蟲 ←

= 面對和處理

Billy Brave was afraid of bugs.
He decided to face up to his fear.

比利 · 布瑞弗怕蟲子。
他決定要面對自己的恐懼。

CREEP UP ON SOMEONE
also SNEAK UP ON SOMEBODY

躡手躡腳在某人後面走

You must creep up on your prey
if you don't want to be heard.

如果你不想被聽到，
一定要躡手躡腳地走在獵物後面。

一些常見的片語動詞：

ACT UP 調皮；任性

ASK so. OVER 邀請某人來

BLOW UP 爆炸；發脾氣

BLOW sth. UP 使某物爆炸；使某物膨脹

BREAK DOWN 故障；失控

BRING sth. ABOUT 引起某事；造成某事

BRING sth. | so. BACK 送回某人或事物

BRING so. DOWN 使某人失望

BRING sth. UP 提出某事

CALL so. BACK 回電給某人

CALL sth. OFF 取消某事

CALL so. UP 打電話給某人

CARRY ON 繼續

CATCH ON 理解；變流行

CHECK sth. OUT 檢視某事物

CHEER so. UP 鼓勵某人

CLEAN sth. | so. UP 清理某人或事物

CLEAR sth. UP 解釋某事

CLOSE sth. DOWN 停業；關閉

COME BACK 回來

COME IN 進來

COME OUT 出櫃；公開發表

COME UP WITH sth. 想出、發明某事物

COUNT ON sth. | so. 依賴某人或事物

CREEP UP ON so. 躡手躡腳在某人後面走

coffin
棺材

EAT AWAY AT

=腐蝕；侵蝕

He killed a mouse and
that is eating away at his conscience.

他殺了一隻老鼠，而那正在侵蝕他的良心。

CUT DOWN ON sth. 縮減某事物

CUT sth. OUT 刪去某事物

CUT sth. UP 切碎

DO sth. OVER 重新做某事

DO sth. | so. UP 重新整裝某人或事物

DRAW sth. TOGETHER 使某事物團結一致

DREAM sth. UP 虛構；編造

DRESS UP 盛裝打扮

DRINK sth. UP 喝盡某物

DROP IN 突然來訪

DROP sth. | so. OFF 讓某人或事物下車

EAT AWAY AT 腐蝕；侵蝕

EAT IN 在家吃飯

EAT OUT 上館子；（對女性）口交

END UP WITH sth. 最後成為某事物

FACE UP TO 面對事實

FALL APART 破裂；破碎

FALL DOWN 失敗

FALL FOR so. 喜歡某人

FIGURE sth. | so. OUT 明白某人或事物

FILL sth. IN 向某人提供詳情

FILL sth. OUT 填寫某事物

FIND sth. OUT 發現某事物

FIX sth. UP 修補好

FIND OUT

= 發現

FALL APART

= 破裂；破碎

A woman with a vase fell down. The woman fell apart.
They used the vase as her funeral urn. It seemed safe.

一名拿著一個花瓶的女人跌倒了。那個女人破了。他們用那個花瓶當作她的骨
灰罈。骨灰罈看起來安全了。

FOLLOW THROUGH 堅持完成

FOOL AROUND 鬼混；胡搞

FREAK OUT 嚇壞

FUCK UP 搞砸

FUCK sth. UP 把某事搞砸

FUCK so. UP 毀掉某人

GIVE sth. UP 放棄某事物

GO ALONG WITH sth. 贊同某事物

GO BACK 回去

GO DOWN 下降

GO ON 繼續

GO OUT 出去

GO UP 上升

GO OVER sth. 察看某事物

GOBBLE DOWN 狼吞虎嚥

GROW UP 長大

HANG OUT 閒蕩；廝混

HANG sth. UP 將某物掛起來

HANG UP 掛電話

HOLD ON 等待；不要掛電話

KEEP AWAY 避免靠近；待在遠處

KEEP ON 繼續

KEEP UP WITH 趕上

LAY sth. DOWN 將某事物放躺下

LAY sth. OUT 計畫某事；花錢

Sweetheart,
it's me!

寶貝，是我。

FREAK OUT
= 嚇壞；行為舉止狂野而且不理智

No matter how much she misses her husband,
every time she sees him she still freaks out.

不管她有多想念她老公，每次見到他她都還是嚇得魂飛魄散。

LEAVE sth. ON 讓某物保持開啟或穿戴著某物

LEAVE sth. | so. OUT 遺漏或排除某人或事物

LET so. DOWN 讓某人失望

LET sth. | so. IN 讓某人或事物進來

LET so. OFF 寬恕某人

LIE DOWN 躺下

LIGHT UP 照亮

LOOK AFTER 照顧

LOOK FOR 尋找

LOOK FORWARD TO 期待

LOOK OUT 小心

LOOK sth. UP 查詢某事物

MISS OUT 失敗

PASS sth. UP 放棄某事物

PAY so. BACK 還某人錢

PAY OFF 帶來好結果

PICK sth. | so. OUT 挑選出某人或事物

PICK UP 有起色；接電話

PICK sth. UP 拾起某物

PICK so. UP 接某人

PISS so. OFF 惹某人惱怒

PLAY AROUND 嬉笑打鬧；亂搞

POINT sth. OUT 指出某事物

PUT sth. AWAY 儲存；歸位

PUT sth. BACK 將某物放回

GOBBLE DOWN

= 狼吞虎嚥

Meryl was starving and didn't feel like cooking so she started gobbling down her beloved husband.

梅若很餓，而且不想煮飯，所以她開始狼吞虎嚥吃掉她親愛的老公。

PISS someone OFF
= 惹某人惱怒

Tamara is a calm girl,
but everything her mother says pisses her off.

塔瑪拉是個淡定的女孩，但她媽媽說的每句話都會讓她很生氣。

PUT so. OFF 讓某人失去興趣或厭惡

PUT sth. OFF 將某事延期

PUT sth. TOGETHER 將某物組合起來

PUT sth. UP 展示某物

RIP so. OFF 敲某人竹槓

RUN INTO so. 偶然遇見某人

SEND sth. BACK 將某物送回

SET sth. UP 安裝、設置某物

SHUT UP 閉嘴

SIGN so. UP 幫某人報名

SIT DOWN 坐下

SLIP UP 弄錯

START sth. OVER 重做某事

STAY UP 熬夜

SWITCH sth. ON 打開某物

TAKE sth. AWAY 拿走某物

TAKE sth. BACK 拿回某物

TAKE sth. IN 了解某事物

TAKE OFF 出發

TAKE sth. OFF 脫掉某物

TAKE so. ON 聘僱某人；迎戰某人

TALK BACK 回嘴

TALK so. INTO 說服某人做

TALK sth. OVER 討論某事

TEAR sth. DOWN | APART 拆掉、毀壞某物

TELL so. OFF 斥責某人

THINK BACK 回想

THINK sth. OVER 三思某事

THINK sth. UP 發想某事

THROW sth. AWAY 丟棄某物

THROW UP 嘔吐

TOUCH sth. UP 修飾某物

TRY sth. ON 試穿某物

TRY sth. OUT 試做某事

TURN sth. DOWN 拒絕某事；將某物關小

TURN so. DOWN 拒絕某人

TURN so. ON 使某人興奮

TURN sth. | so. INTO 將某人或事物變成

TURN so. OFF 使某人不感興趣或感到被冒犯

TURN sth. ON 打開某物

TURN so. ON 使某人興奮

TURN OUT 結果變成

TURN UP 突然出現

TURN sth. UP 將某物增大

WATCH OUT 注意

WAKE so. UP 叫醒某人

WORK sth. OFF 售出；去除

WORK OUT 解決；運動

WRITE sth. DOWN 寫下某事物

TRY SOMETHING **ON**

= 試穿某物

He tried the gabardine on.
It was perfect for his exhibitionist habits.

他試穿那件長袍。對於他的暴露狂習慣真是太適合了。

PHRASAL VERBS WITH GET

get 的片語動詞

有些片語動詞會有很多種不同的意思，特別是用 get 這個字的片語動詞。

GET ALONG

與⋯⋯相處

GET BACK AT SOMEONE
= 報仇

我會找你報仇的。

GET BACK
= 從某地回來
= 報仇

GET BACK INTO
= 重新投入某事

GET BACK TO
= 回應聯繫
= 在中斷後又回頭開始做某事

GET BACK TOGETHER

= 復合

GET BACK INTO

=重回；重新投入某事

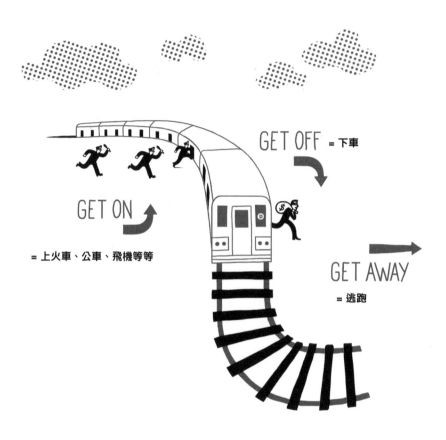

GET OFF = 下車

GET ON = 上火車、公車、飛機等等

GET AWAY = 逃跑

GET ON – GET OFF – GET AWAY

While the policemen were getting on the train to catch Billy Prank, he got off. Finally, he got away.

警方上火車要去抓比利‧普蘭克時，他又下車了。最後就讓他逃跑了。

其他用法

GET ON

= 上火車、公車、飛機等等
= 繼續做某事
= 年老

GET OFF

= 下車
= 躲過處罰
= 下班
= 開始一段旅程
= 掛電話
= 到高潮

* When Patrick added the last stamp to his 33rd album of stamps, he got off.

派崔克在他第三十三本集郵冊裡加進最後一張郵票時,他高潮了。

GET AWAY

= 脫逃
= 去度假或短程旅行
= 移動、離開一個地方

GET OUT OF

= 拿開；遠離

He always tries to get out of doing the cha cha cha.
But her charm prevents it.

他總是試著遠離恰恰，但是她的魅力阻止了這件事。

GET something ACROSS

= 傳達某事

GET AHEAD

= 進步

GET BY

= 勉強過活

GET OUT OF something

= 遠離某事物（車子、計程車、地方）

GET something OUT OF something

= 從某事物中獲利

GET THROUGH (with)

= 完成

GET TOGETHER (with someone)

= （和某人）見面

GET UP

= 起床

lesson

Modals & Similar Expressions

[情態動詞和類似表達語]

情態動詞和類似的表達語有：
can, could, be able to（以上均為「能夠」），
should（應該）, ought to（應該）, had better（最好），
have to, have got to, must（以上均為「必須」），
may（可能）, might（可能）, would（會）, will（會）．

這些助動詞是用來表達以下的意思：
能力、忠告、必要性、禁止、推測、
未來可能性、允許、要求和建議。

現在式的情態動詞後面都是接原型動詞。

這些動詞只有一種型態，所以第三人稱單數時不加s。
She <u>must</u> have been lost. 她一定是迷路了。

be able to（能夠）, have to（必須）或 have got to（必須），
不是情態動詞，所以就必須用變化型。
She <u>has to</u> be lost. 她必定得迷路。

can、**could** 和 **be able to** 用來表達能力。

can't、**couldn't** 和 **not be able to** 用來表達沒有辦法。

can 用在現在式。
I can sing, play the guitar and ride a unicycle at the same time.
我可以同時唱歌、彈吉他和騎獨輪車。
I can't teach you. I don't know how I do it.
我不能教你。我不知道我怎麼做到的。

———————————————

could 用在過去式。
I could laugh at my classmates without regrets when I was child.
我還小的時候，可以毫無歉意地取笑我的同學。
I couldn't understand English before I read this book.
在閱讀這本書之前，我看不懂英文。

———————————————

be able to 可以用在所有動詞時態。
be able to 的現在式或過去式比 can 或 could 正式。
用 be able to 的時候，要根據每個動詞時態來使用正確的變化形。

I'm able to follow your orders, boss. 老闆，我能遵守你的命令。
She wasn't able to come with me. 她沒法跟我一起來。
Will you be able to go to Berlin next summer? 明年夏天你能去柏林嗎？
I like being able to do what I like. 我喜歡能夠做我喜歡做的事。

should、ought to 和 had better 或
shouldn't、ought not 和 had better not 用來給忠告。

should 和 ought to 指的是同樣的事，但 should 比較常見。
這些動詞可以用在現在式和未來式。
You should leave him. 你應該離開他。
We shouldn't forget they are humans. 我們不應該忘了他們是人類。
You ought to just be yourself. 你應該做自己就好了。

ought to 的否定是 ought not，不加 to。
She ought not watch this movie. She'll be afraid tonight.
她不應該看那部電影，她今晚會很怕。

---

should 用來詢問建議。
Should I quit my job? 我應該辭職嗎？

---

had better 用來推薦：
You'd better stop smoking. 你最好戒菸。

用作極度希望或暗示性的威脅：
He'd better not be having an affair. 他最好別搞外遇。

用來警告別人：
You'd better not run so much, this road is dangerous!
你最好別跑那麼多，這條路很危險！

to give ADVICE
給建議

You ought to just be yourself.

你應該做自己就好了。

to express NECESSITY
表達必要性

have to、**have got to** 和 **must** 用來表達義務或必要性。

---

have to 比較常用於一般性的義務。
have got to 表達較強烈的情緒。
have got to 用在對話和非正式書寫中。
People <u>have to</u> pay taxes. 人民必須繳稅。
You<u>'ve got to</u> see this clown. He's really funny.
你一定要看看這個小丑。他真的很好笑。

---

must 和 **have to** 比較常用在特定和個人的義務。
have to 可以用在所有語境中。
I <u>must</u> be on time at work, it's my first day.
我一定要準時上班，今天是我第一天上班。
I <u>have to</u> be on time at work, it's my first day.
我得準時上班，今天是我第一天上班。

must 用在正式的使用說明和手冊。
Employees <u>must</u> wash hands before returning to work.
員工必須洗手後再返回工作崗位。

---

have got to 和 **must** 是使用現在式和未來式。
have to 可以用在各種動詞時態。
She <u>has to</u> study a lot in order to pass the exam.
為了通過考試，她得相當用功。
She <u>will have to</u> study a lot in order to pass the exam.
為了通過考試，她將得相當用功。

have to 和 **must** 也可以用在強烈的建議。
You <u>have to</u> see a shrink, you're mad! 你得看心理醫生，你瘋了！
You <u>must</u> eat more! 你得多吃點！

You must be nice to your classmates.
You mustn't hit them.

你一定要對同學友善，不可以打他們。

But we have to win everyone's respect.

但我們必須贏得所有人的尊重。

to express NONNECESSITY
表達不必要性

don't have to 用來表達某件事是不必要的。可以用各種動詞時態。

You don't have to do this right now.
你不必現在做這個。

We didn't have to be nice. 我們不必客氣。

I won't have to get up early any more because I've been fired.
我再也不用早起了，因為我被炒魷魚了。

to express PROHIBITION
表達禁止

mustn't 用來表達禁止。
可以用現在式和未來式。

You mustn't hit people. 你不可以打人。

You mustn't drive without a license.
你不可以無照駕駛。

can't 也可以用來表達禁止。

You can't drive without a license.
你不可以無照駕駛。

to express ASSUMPTIONS
表達假設

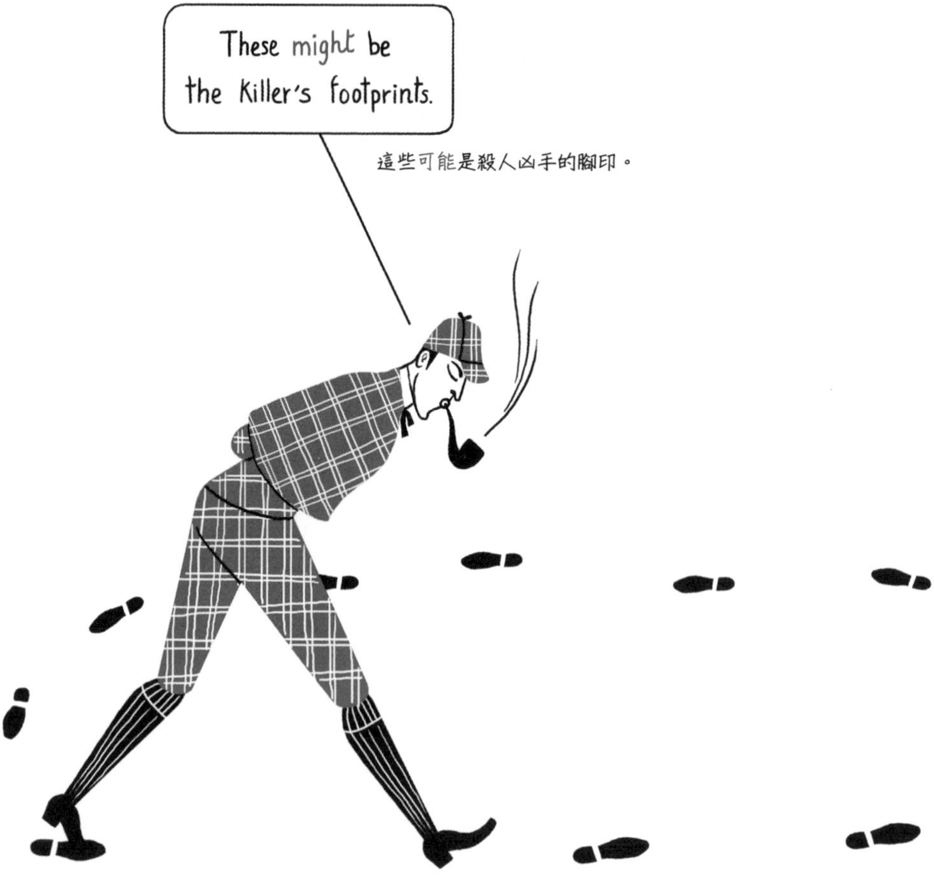

must、have to、have got to、may、might、could
和 can't、couldn't、mustn't、may not、might not 可以用來表達假設。

這些情態動詞表達確定或疑問,用於現在式。

must、have to 和 have got to 表達的是百分之百的確定。
may、might 和 could 表達較弱的確定。

_____

can't 和 couldn't 表達百分之百的確定不行。
mustn't 表達弱一點點的確定不行。
may not 和 might not 表達更弱的確定不行。

_____

to talk about
FUTURE POSSIBILITY
關於未來的可能性

may、might 和 could 用來表達可能性。

---

may、might 和 could 是相同的。

The store <u>may</u> open at 10 tomorrow. 那家店可能明天早上開門。
The store <u>might</u> open at 10 tomorrow. 那家店可能明天早上開門。
The store <u>could</u> open at 10 tomorrow. 那家店可能明天早上開門。

MAY NOT 和 MIGHT NOT 表達某事不會發生的可能性。

The store <u>may not</u> open at 10. 那家店可能不會在十點開門。
The store <u>might not</u> open at 10. 那家店可能不會在十點開門。

**may 和 might 通常不會用在關於可能性的疑問句中。
其他可以用的用法有:**

Will the store open at 10? 那家店會在十點開門嗎?
Do you think the store will be open at 10? 你認為那家店會在十點開門嗎?

我可以在這裡抽菸嗎？

to ask
PERMISSION
詢問許可

may 和 **can** 用來詢問許可。

may 比較正式。
<u>May</u> I smoke here? 我可以在這裡抽菸嗎？
No, but you <u>may</u> smoke outside. 不可以，不過你可以在外面抽。
can 比較口語。
<u>Can</u> I smoke here, buddy? 兄弟，我可以在這抽菸嗎？
You <u>can</u> smoke outside, my dear. 你可以在外面抽，親愛的。

to make
REQUESTS
提出要求

would、**could**、**will** 和 **can** 用來提出要求。

would 和 could 較正式。
Would you please bring me a coffee? 可以請你幫我帶杯咖啡嗎？
Could you do my homework? 你可以幫我做功課嗎？

WILL 或 CAN 可以用在非正式口語中。
Will you tell me a story? 你可以講個故事給我聽嗎？
Can you leave me alone? 你可以讓我清靜一下嗎？

to offer
SUGGESTIONS
提出建議

would you like、**shall** 和 **should** 用來提出建議。
shall 只用在第一人稱單數和複數。
Would you like a beer? 你要啤酒嗎？
Shall we take a walk? 我們去散步吧？
Should we go out tonight? 我們今晚是不是應該出去？

非正式的情況用：
let's、why don't we 和 how about
Let's take a walk! 我們散個步吧！
Why don't we go out? 我們何不出去呢？
How about getting something to drink? 來杯喝的怎麼樣？

[附加問句]
QUESTiON
TAgs

附加問句是句尾較短的問句，用於確認。
It's a beautiful day, isn't it? 今天天氣真好，不是嗎？

和用來詢問資訊或要求協助。
You don't know where the station is, do you? 你不知道車站在哪裡，對不對？

附加問句的句型是：
句子的**助動詞** + 句子的**主詞**

肯定句要用否定的附加問句。
She dances very well, <u>doesn't she?</u> 她舞跳得很好，對不對？
You're tired, <u>aren't you?</u> 你很累了，對不對？

否定句要用肯定的附加問句。
You don't like me, <u>do you?</u> 你不喜歡我，對不對？

祈使句的附加問句通常是用 will。
Shut up, <u>will you?</u> 閉嘴，好嗎？

lesson 15

條件句描述的情況和環境是有因果關係的。
如果現在有某一個特定的情況，則會有一個特定的結果發生。

條件句是由兩個子句構成：
if子句和結果子句

你可以用 if 子句作為條件句的開頭，用結果子句作開頭也可以。
意思是一樣的。

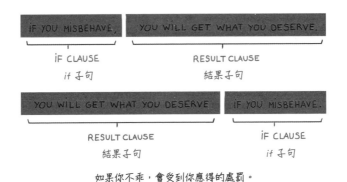

如果你不乖，會受到你應得的處罰。

注意，如果 if 子句在先，兩個子句之間要加**逗號**。

ZERO CONDITIONAL
零條件句

---

if + 現在簡單式……，……現在簡單式……

If you heat water to 100 degrees, it boils.
如果你把水加熱到一百度，水就會滾。

IF YOU HEAT WATER TO 100 DEGREES
CELSIUS, IT BOILS.

如果你把水加熱到攝氏一百度，水就會滾。

用在一般事實。

通常你可以用 when，而不必用 if。
When you heat water to 100 degrees celsius,
it boils.
當你把水加熱到攝氏一百度，水就會滾。

2

用在**習慣和總是發生的事**。

你可以在 if 子句中用現在簡單式
或現在進行式。

---

if + **現在進行式**……，……**現在簡單式**……
If Susan is feeling happy, she dances.
如果蘇珊覺得快樂，她就會跳舞。

IF SUSAN FEELS INSPIRED,
SHE SINGS.

如果蘇珊覺得靈感來了，
她就會唱歌。

3

依據特定情況用來給**指令或邀請**，可
以用 if 子句加祈使句。

---

if ……**現在簡單式**……，……**祈使句**……
If you are free, come over for dinner.
如果你有空，過來吃晚餐。

COME OVER FOR DINNER
IF YOU ARE FREE.

如果你有空，過來吃晚餐。

FIRST CONDITIONAL
第一條件句

---

if +現在簡單式……，……未來式……

If you love me, you will stay with me. 如果你愛我，就會伴我左右。

第一條件句用來講未來的可能性。

> **IF YOU LOVE ME, YOU WILL ALWAYS STAY WITH ME.**
> 如果你愛找，就會永遠伴找左右。

> **IF YOU ARE FEELING BORED, I WILL SING YOU A SONG.**
> 如果你覺得無聊，找就唱首歌給你聽。

除了現在簡單式，你也可以用其他的現在式：

現在進行式： *If you <u>are feeling</u> bored, I'll sing you a song.* 如果你覺得無聊，我就唱首歌給你聽。

現在完成式： *If you <u>have</u> already <u>eaten</u> chicken today,*
I'll give you chicken tomorrow. 如果你今天已經吃過雞肉了，我就明天再給你雞肉。

現在完成進行式： *If you <u>have been watching</u> TV, I'll throw it away.*
如果你一直看電視，我就把電視丟掉。

IF SHE GETS DISTRACTED, I CAN ESCAPE.

如果有人分散她的注意力,我就可以逃跑了。

UNLESS HE SUDDENLY LEAVES, I WILL BE ABLE TO ESCAPE UNNOTICED.

除非他突然離去,不然我就可以逃跑而不被發現。

will是情態動詞。其他**情態動詞**則表達不同的意思。

If she gets distracted, I <u>can</u> escape | I <u>could</u> escape | I <u>might</u> be able to escape.

如果有人分散她的注意力,我就可以逃跑了。 | 我就能逃跑了。 | 我就可能可以逃跑了。

SECOND CONDITIONAL
第二條件句

---

if + 過去簡單式……，……would + 原型動詞……

If men liked her, she would be happy. 如果男人喜歡她，她就會快樂了。

第二條件句用來講假設的情況。

IF MEN LIKED ME,
I WOULD BE HAPPY.

如果男人喜歡我，
我就會快樂了。

假設的情況有：

假想情境
If I were married, I would make my husband the happiest man in the world.
如果我結婚了，我會讓我老公成為世界上最快樂的男人。

不可能的
If I were a man, I would like hairy women.
如果我是個男人，我會喜歡毛髮多的女人。

不太可能發生的
If I had a lover, I would tickle him with my hair.
如果我有愛人，我會用我的頭髮搔他癢。

除了過去簡單式，你還可以用：
過去進行式： *If you <u>were looking</u> for a lover, I might be available.*
如果你在找愛人，我可能可以。

除了would，你還可以用：
could: *If I were wealthy, I <u>could</u> buy everything I need.*
如果我很有錢，就能買所有我需要的東西了。
might: *If I shaved off my beard, I <u>might</u> be able to get married.*
如果我刮掉我的鬍子，我可能就能結婚了。

THIRD CONDITIONAL
第三條件句

---

if + 過去完成式……，……would have + 過去分詞……
If I had lived longer, I would have loved much more.
如果我能活久一點，我就能愛得更多一點。
第三條件句用來講過去的假設情況，即過去沒發生的事。

除了 would have，你還可以用：

should have: *If he had hurt your feelings, he <u>should have</u> apologized.*
如果他傷了你的心，他當時應該要道歉。

could have: *If I had realized it sooner, I <u>could have</u> gotten together with the woman who brings me flowers.* 如果我早點發現，我就能跟那個送我花的女人在一起了。

might have: *If I I had been luckier, I <u>might have</u> succeeded in life.*
如果我更幸運一點，我的人生可能就會有所成就了。

NATASHA
TSKANSKAYA
03.17.1921
12.15.2001

I HAVE
NOTHING
FURTHER
TO SAY.

.13.1924
.20.2000

IF I HAD REALIZED IT SOONER, I COULD HAVE GOTTEN TOGETHER WITH THE WOMAN WHO BRINGS ME FLOWERS EVERY WEEK.

如果我早點發現，我就
能跟那個每個星期都送我
花的女人在一起了。

IF I HAD KNOWN, I WOULDN'T HAVE WORRIED OVER BULLSHIT.

KACHKO
12.06.1934-05.11.2001

BORIS
ZHIK
MAY 23.1949-DEC. 21 1989

如果我早知道，就不會
擔心狗屁倒灶的事了。

[If 還是 Whether?]
If or Whether?

I WONDER WHETHER I SHOULD HAVE ADDED A LITTLE MORE POISON TO HIS TEA.

找在想是不是應該多加
一點毒藥在他的茶裡。

if 和 whether 相似，但有一些不同之處。

if 用來：
表達一個條件。
在條件句中，if 引導條件。
If something annoys you, look for a solution.
如果有事情讓你煩惱，就找個解決方法吧。

---

whether 用來：
提出兩種選擇。
I wonder whether I should have added a little more poison to his tea.
我在想是不是應該多加一點毒藥在他的茶裡。
(=Should I have added more poison or not? 我應該多加點毒藥，還是不應該呢？)

可用在介系詞後面。
We argued about whether I behaved rudely towards him.
我們爭論我是否對他很無禮。

用在不定詞前。
I've been thinking about whether to get rid of everything that annoys me.
我一直在想是不是要擺脫讓我煩惱的所有事物。

---

whether 或 if 都可以用在：
回答是或非的問題。
She wondered whether | if he was right. 她在想他是不是對的。
問題是：*Was he right?*

用在 whether | if... or... 的結構。
I would like to know whether | if the problem is me or him.
我想知道問題是在我還是他。

lesson 16

IDioMS
[諺語]

諺語是一些從字面上看不出涵意的用語，
而且不一定會遵守一般的語言模式。

It's Raining Cats and Dogs

傾盆大雨。

HiT THe SaCk

上床睡覺。

HAVE A FROG IN ONE'S THROAT
= 聲音沙啞，通常是因為恐懼。

BE BENT OUT OF SHAPE
= 氣急敗壞。

BARK UP THE WRONG TREE
= 找錯目標白費力氣。

MAKE ENDS MEET
= 收支平衡；量入為出。

LAUGH ALL THE WAY TO THE BANK
= （做不被看好的事而）發財得意。

BE ON THE EDGE OF ONE'S SEAT
= 興奮不已；坐立難安。

HAVE A SEAT
= 坐下。

DO YOUR BEST
= 盡力。

DON'T GIVE ME ANY LIP!
= 不要頂嘴！

MoNkeY SeE,

MONKEY DO

有樣學樣。

COUNT ON SOMEONE
= 依賴某人。

BE ON THE FENCE
= 難以抉擇。

STEW IN ONE'S OWN JUICES
= 自食惡果。

GET ONE'S FOOT IN THE DOOR
= 踏出第一步。

BE UNDER THE WEATHER
= 身體不舒服。

DROP A HINT
= 給個暗示。

SWEAT BULLETS
= 擔心不已。

IN GOOD SHAPE
= 很健康。

WITH BELLS ON
= 熱切地；樂意地。

LOOK LIKE A MILLION DOLLARS

看起來容光煥發。

TALK CRAP

也可說TALK SHIT
=罵人或說謊，或同時兩者都有。

BE MILES AWAY

=心不在焉。

BE ALL EARS

=洗耳恭聽。

HANG IN THERE

= 撐下去。

EVERY CLOUD HAS A SILVER LINING

= 撥雲見日。

HAVE A BLAST

= 玩得盡興。

TIT FOR TAT
AN EYE FOR AN EYE | A TOOTH FOR A TOOTH

= 以牙還牙。

BE GREEN WITH ENVY

= 非常嫉妒。

SHAKE IN ONE'S SHOES

= 嚇得發抖。

HIT THE BULL'S-EYE

= 正中靶心；切中要害。

GET OFF ON THE WRONG FOOT

= 出師不利。

ONE'S CUP OF TEA

= 合某人胃口。

RACE AGAINST THE CLOCK

= 跟時間賽跑。

JOG SOMEONE'S MEMORY

= 喚起某人的記憶。

MONEY TALKS

= 有錢能使鬼推磨。

DRIVE SOMEONE TO DISTRACTION

= 令人心煩意亂。

HAVE BUTTERFLIES IN ONE'S STOMACH

= 忐忑不安。

CATCH RED-HANDED

= 逮個正著。

GO NUTS | GO BANANAS

= 瘋了。

MAKE UP ONE'S MIND

= 決定。

KEEP ONE'S CHIN UP

= 不氣餒。

WHEN PIGS FLY
WHEN HELL FREEZES OVER

= 不可能。

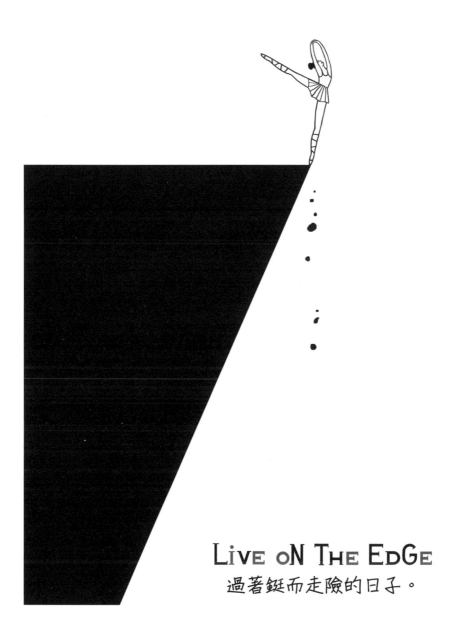

LIVE ON THE EDGE

過著鋌而走險的日子。

Like
Two Peas in a Pod

一模一樣。

CRY OVER SPILT MILK

= 為已無法挽救的局面懊悔難過。

KEEP ONE'S EYE ON THE BALL

= 對周遭發生的事維持警戒。

CHANGE ONE'S MIND

= 改變心意。

MY LIPS ARE SEALED

= 守口如瓶。

BEAT ONESELF UP

= 自責。

CUT CORNERS

= 抄捷徑。

(I, you, he...) CAN'T STAND

= 無法忍受。

GET INTO A JAM

= 陷入困境。

GET OUT OF A JAM

= 擺脫困境。

NOT SLEEP A WINK
= 沒闔過眼。

SLEEP LIKE A LOG
= 熟睡得像塊木頭。

WORK LIKE A DOG
= 做牛做馬地幹活。

HIT THE ROAD
= 上路。

BREAK A LEG!
= 祝你好運！

GIVE SOMEBODY THE EVIL EYE
= 怒瞪某人。

SMELL A RAT
= 事有蹊蹺。

BE IN HOT WATER
= 處境困難。

A DIME A DOZEN
= 不值錢。

YOU BET!
= 沒錯！不客氣！

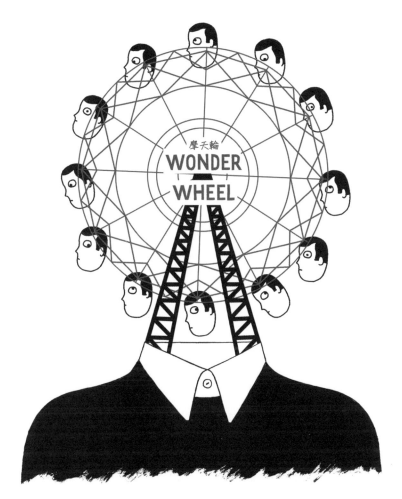

MY HeaD iS SpiNNiNG

頭昏腦脹。

lesson

17

USEFUL

EXPRESSIONS

[實用語]

生存必備的字彙。

用來請求原諒。

CHEERS!
乾杯!

BLESS YOU
祝福你

AH-CHOO

敲杯敬酒前的常見用語。

某人打噴嚏時可用。

WATCH OUT!
小心!

要某人注意可能有危險。

HURRY UP!
趕快!

堅持要某人快點做某事。

用來引起某人注意。

用在第一次會面別人時。

要某人再講一次。

INSULTS

髒話

冒犯他人的語言。

Imbecile
= 笨蛋。

Imbecile

Motherfucker

Motherfucker
= 不要臉的傢伙。

Asshole

Asshole
= 混蛋。

Asshisser
=馬屁精（也可說
asslicker）。

Bitch
= 賤人。

Fuck off
= 滾開。

CONNECTED SPEECH
[連用語]

在口語或非正式寫作中，將兩個字連用發音成一個字。

My mother's **gonna** drive me crazy.

我媽快要把我逼瘋了。
= GOING TO

You **gotta** be careful with me.

你得要提防著我。
= HAVE GOT TO

I **wanna** kiss you.

我想親你。
= WANT TO

We **woulda** won if they hadn't.

如果他們沒贏就是我們贏了。
= WOULD HAVE

It **coulda** been worse.

有可能更糟。
= COULD HAVE

She **shoulda** waxed her moustache.

她應該要拔掉她的八字鬍的。
= SHOULD HAVE

ACRONYMS
[縮寫]

由一組字的首字母構成的字，寫作和口語英文中很常見。

TGIF！

感謝老天星期五了！

常見縮寫：

TGIF 感謝老天星期五了
Thank God It's Friday

ASAP 盡快
As Soon As Possible

FYI 供您參考
For Your Information

LOL 大笑
Laughing Out Loud

AKA 又叫做
Also Known As

ID 身分證明
Identification

BTW 順道一提
By The Way

XOXO 親親抱抱
Hugs And Kissess

FAQs 常見問與答
Frequently Asked Questions

RIP 安息
Rest In Peace

SIORI MASA ENRIQUE ME JON NICHOLAS ? MARC ROBERT

acknowledgements

致謝

感謝偷了我的包包和畫冊的小偷,我這些插畫多半都在畫冊裡,
小偷後來又把畫冊丟到垃圾桶裡讓我找到了。
謝謝圖片中的這些人,我在紐約那段特別的時光裡有他們陪伴。
還要謝謝阿諾,現在還陪伴著我。

http://www.booklife.com.tw   reader@mail.eurasian.com.tw

圓神文叢 161

英文給它有點難，我靠畫畫搞定它

作　　者／露琪·古提耶雷茲（Luci Gutierrez）
譯　　者／歐罷
發 行 人／簡志忠
出 版 者／圓神出版社有限公司
地　　址／台北市南京東路四段50號6樓之1
電　　話／（02）2579-6600·2579-8800·2570-3939
傳　　真／（02）2579-0338·2577-3220·2570-3636
郵撥帳號／18598712　圓神出版社有限公司
總 編 輯／陳秋月
主　　編／林慈敏
責任編輯／林慈敏
美術編輯／黃一涵
行銷企畫／涂姿宇·吳幸芳
印務統籌／林永潔
監　　印／高榮祥
校　　對／莊淑涵·林慈敏
排　　版／陳采淇
經 銷 商／叩應股份有限公司
法律顧問／圓神出版事業機構法律顧問　蕭雄淋律師
印　　刷／祥峰印刷廠
2014年5月　初版
2019年10月　20刷

ENGLISH IS NOT EASY
by Luci Gutierrez
Copyright © 2013 by Luci Gutierrez
Published in agreement with MB Agencia Literaria SL, through The Grayhawk Agency
Complex Chinese translation copyrights © 2014 by Eurasian Press
All rights reserved.

定價 330 元　　　　ISBN 978-986-133-498-1
◎本書如有缺頁、破損、裝訂錯誤，請寄回本公司調換

每一本書，都是有靈魂的。

這個靈魂，不但是作者的靈魂，

也是曾經讀過這本書，與它一起生活、一起夢想的人留下來的靈魂。

——《風之影》

想擁有圓神、方智、先覺、究竟、如何、寂寞的閱讀魔力：

◪ 請至鄰近各大書店洽詢選購。

◪ 圓神書活網，24小時訂購服務

　　免費加入會員‧享有優惠折扣：www.booklife.com.tw

◪ 郵政劃撥訂購：

　　服務專線：02-25798800　讀者服務部

　　郵撥帳號及戶名：18598712　圓神出版社有限公司

國家圖書館出版品預行編目資料

英文給它有點難，我靠畫畫搞定它 / 露琪‧古提耶雷茲（Luci Gutierrez）著；
歐寵 譯. -- 初版. -- 臺北市：圓神，2014.05
336 面；17×21公分. --（圓神文叢；161）
譯自：English is not easy : a guide to the language
ISBN 978-986-133-498-1（平裝）
1.英語 2.語法 3.插畫

805.16　　　　　　　　　　　　　　　　　　　　　103004974